THE WOLF AND THE SHEEP

WOLF #1

PENELOPE SKY

Hartwick Publishing

The Wolf and the Sheep

Copyright © 2019 by Penelope Sky

CONTENTS

1

MAVERICK

As a young boy, I used to stand in this very spot.

Right in the doorway, neither in the bedroom or outside it, I used to blend in with the shadows and stare at my father's back. He'd been taller than me most of my life, so I looked up to him—literally.

He always had the same routine as he stood in front of his vanity. First, he folded his sleeves back and buttoned them. Then the cuff links were added—one of the many pairs he owned. My mother always gifted him a new set on his birthday, finding something sleek he would be proud to wear.

Once the cuff links were secured, he pulled the watch onto his wrist. White gold and flashy, it contrasted against the dark colors he usually wore. His suits were always black or blue, never tan or silver. His change in wardrobe seemed to occur after the worst day of his life came to pass.

His silver wedding ring sat on the vanity where it'd been every day for a year. He always stared at it for a long time, as if he were considering putting it on again.

When I was a child, it was something he never put on—because he'd always been wearing it.

But now he didn't know what to do with it.

He straightened in front of the mirror and admired himself, his shirt still tight on his muscular arms. Sunlight had made his skin tanned and slightly weathered like worn-out leather, but he still possessed the resilience of a young man. Veins stretched from the tops of his hands and up his arms, protruding from the tight skin. He was tall, a mountain in my eyes, but he'd shrunk down as gravity worked against him all these decades.

Now I was taller than him.

Stronger than him.

But not smarter than him.

Our lives had never been the same since that terrible day one year ago.

We had never been the same.

He lifted his gaze and met mine in the mirror. "Yes?"

When I was a child, he never noticed me because I was too short. But I was a man now...and I'd been a man a long time. Made in his likeness, I possessed his strength, his might. And unfortunately, I inherited all of his flaws—his coldness and his cruelty.

His deep voice reverberated against the wall, filling every room in the old castle like he was the original king who'd ruled it centuries ago. Life hadn't been kind to him, so he'd gradually darkened like the stone that comprised the walls of this enormous keep. It'd been the perfect playground for a family of four. But now that he was just a man of one...it was a large coffin.

I stepped out of the darkness of the hallway and entered

his bedroom, the air reeking of solitude. I could feel the lone-liness he never showed, the tears he never shed. "You asked for me." Like a good son, I obeyed my father even as a grown man. His lack of affection always disappointed me, but I respected him all the same.

After his watch was secured, he rolled down his sleeves and eyed his wedding ring once again, as if he were tempted to put it on and travel back in time, to fix the mistakes it was too late to correct.

He turned around, his chin up and his shoulders strong. "I have a meeting—and you're coming with me."

THE CAR STOPPED at the black iron gates, an image of a stallion carved into the bars. Once the security detail allowed us through, we drove up the gravel and approached the three-story estate that sat on prime Tuscan land. Summer was just around the corner, so dusk came late. It was almost eight o'clock, and the sky was still tinted with hues of pink and purple.

The car circled the large fountain in the center, and I admired the ancient cobblestone that made up the walls of the mansion. With curved archways for the windows and ivy that grew up along the sides, it was clearly a family legacy. Homes like this were passed down through generations, starting with ancient ancestral royalty until the present time. It was unlikely this property had been purchased in the last five years.

I tilted my face toward my father, keeping my eyes on our surroundings at the same time. "What are we doing here?"

My father glanced at his watch. "Your guess is as good as mine." His door was opened, and he stepped out.

I got out as well, and we were escorted inside, entering an enormous archway with a stunning chandelier. Artwork from the 1800s was on the walls, mostly landscapes of lilies and ponds.

The men guided us farther inside, bringing us into an enormous dining room lined with more historical paintings and sculptures. I'd grown up with money, so I knew what different levels existed. My family made their fortune through legal and illegal means. But judging from this magnitude, this family was aristocracy.

We sat down at the long table, a table that could easily seat fifty people for dinner.

I couldn't even name fifty people that I liked.

The men left the room.

My father sat at the head of the table. With a perfectly straight back and an aggressive nature, he was ready for whatever this meeting would involve.

I was still in the dark about everything. This could be a new client. This could be an enemy. This could be a friend. I really had no idea. "Who are we meeting?" My voice was minimized by the size of the room, the high ceilings that held several chandeliers. Instead of windows showing the outside world, it was just painting after painting.

"Martin Chatel." My father continued to stare straight ahead, his fingers resting on the mahogany of the table. As if he were the one who had called the meeting, he sat with perfect poise, still as a statue.

Chatel. I recognized the family name.

French.

They had family relations all over Europe, a bloodline that traced back through kings. The wealth displayed on every wall had been respectfully inherited through superiority. My father was no longer in the criminal hemisphere, so I had no idea what our purpose was tonight. Unless he'd had a change of heart? "And why are we here?"

"Martin said he had an offer I wouldn't refuse."

I didn't ask any more questions, knowing my father's patience for talking had officially expired. My eyes moved to a painting on the wall, a portrait that stood out from all the others because it clearly didn't belong there. Displaying a modern hand and new paint, it was a piece of art created recently, not hundreds of years ago. A young woman with brown hair the same color as this rich table sat in front of a dressing room mirror, gazing at her reflection as she prepared for whatever production she was about to perform. A brush was on the table, along with makeup supplies. She wore a tight dress and a diamond necklace. She was young, with rosy cheeks, painted lips, and eyes so blue, they were each their own ocean. She looked directly into the mirror, directly into the admirer of the piece. She seemed intelligent but innately innocent. She seemed kind but also callous.

But most of all, she was beautiful.

It was rare for the beauty of a woman to impress me, but I did appreciate art. The piece was special because it seemed so vulnerable, as if she didn't want to sit for the painting but was forced to. I saw two sides to her—a young girl and a woman.

There was nothing else in the room more entertaining, so my eyes stayed with the painting until our host joined us.

Martin Chatel entered the room, thin and pale. He

seemed like a man who hadn't seen the sunlight in years, either because he was too busy working to make the time— or he preferred darkness. He sat at the opposite head of the table, even though that meant he was several feet away.

I ignored the interesting painting and stared at the man who had summoned us here.

Martin drummed his fingers against the table somewhat anxiously. "Caspian, it's been a while."

"It wouldn't feel that way if I had a drink in my hand." My father's presence was suffocating at times. He could saturate your mind with words, choke you with his derisive looks. He was a strong and fearless man—which made him terrifying.

Martin paused before he released a chuckle. "This isn't that kind of occasion."

"I've never heard of an occasion where drinking wasn't involved. Even at my wife's funeral, I drank like an ox." My father stared at Martin across the table, burning him with his coffee-colored eyes, before gesturing to me. "This is my son, Maverick."

Martin looked at me, his eyes sizing me up. He stared at my blue suit, my well-kept hair, and the priceless watch that sat on my wrist. When he was satisfied with his assessment, he turned back to my father. "I know who he is."

I suspected my father brought me to these meetings because he wasn't as focused as he used to be. Now he was more reckless, more unpredictable. I seemed to ground him, to give him a second sight. Most importantly, I was stronger. Age had made my father weak, but youth made me limber and strong.

My father tapped his knuckles against the wood. "So, what is this offer I won't refuse, Martin? You summoned us here without offering us a drink, so you better not have completely wasted my time."

"And mine." Sometimes my presence was dwarfed by my father's, but make no mistake, I was definitely his son. I was just as cold and just as calculating. Ever since we ended our illegal activities, I'd been living a quiet life running the legitimate family business. But prior to that, I made heads roll.

Martin eyed us both, wearing a collared shirt and tie that seemed wrinkled. The clothes also appeared too big, as if they belonged to someone several sizes larger. For a man dripping with wealth, he looked dirty and poor—as if he belonged on the street. "I can get Ramon for you."

That name was cursed in our house.

The second the name was whispered across the dining table, my father and I turned abruptly still, our bodies shutting down but our hearts beating faster. There was no greater enemy to our family, no worse crime ever committed.

I turned to my father and saw the sickly expression on his face, the way his skin stretched over his skeleton as every muscle tightened to the most extensive degree. His eyes steamed like frothed coffee, and his hand immediately tightened into a fist.

Martin continued to watch our reactions, knowing he'd said the perfect words to entice us both.

"Your offer better be concrete." My father forced the words out of his mouth, but his throat was so tight that his words were raspy. There was too much rage for him to hold back, too much anger that surged through his body like a current.

"It is." Martin closed his eyes for a moment, like he was fighting a sudden bout of fatigue. "I can tell you exactly where he's going to be in three weeks. I'll give you everything you need to take him down."

My father had never given up his search for Ramon—for the man who killed my mother. My father's hand shook slightly on the table, like he was picturing Ramon's death that very moment. Ever since my mother had been raped and killed, my father had been a ghost. Now he had no purpose for living, and all he cared about was burning Ramon alive. He breathed hard before he spoke his next words. "In exchange for what?" There was no price my father wouldn't pay.

There was no price I wouldn't pay either. We'd spent the last year trying to track down the man who murdered my mother, an innocent person who had nothing to do with business. He snatched her while she was out shopping and did terrible things to her. It made me sick every time I thought about it, and I was glad she was dead...just so she wasn't suffering anymore.

When my father didn't get his answer quickly enough, he repeated his question. "In exchange for what, Martin? If they find out you were the rat, you'll be done. So, what could possibly be worth the risk?"

It didn't matter what Martin asked for—we would give him anything. My father would never find peace until Ramon was tortured and killed. I needed it for vengeance. This man hurt my family—and I would kill his entire family line in retaliation.

Martin shifted his gaze to me. "I want Maverick to marry my daughter."

I assumed he would ask for a fortune. Or ask us to kill some of his biggest enemies. The last thing I expected was a marriage proposal.

My father didn't flinch. "Done."

I did a double take, shocked my father had consented to this so easily. "I didn't agree to that."

"But you will." My father challenged me with his gaze, telling me to be silent and accept the terms.

But I refused. "No." I held his gaze and didn't care about my appearance of disrespect. I was willing to lay down my life for his, to do whatever was necessary to avenge my mother, but marry someone? That was a ridiculous request. I turned back to Martin. "What kind of deal is that? Why would you even want me to marry her?"

"It doesn't matter," Father snapped. "If that's what he wants, then fine."

I turned to Martin. "Explain. Now." I wasn't the kind of man a father would want for his daughter. I wasn't respectful or understanding. I'd killed people for little to no reason at all. I wasn't romantic or gentle.

Martin looked me in the eye and blinked a few times. "Things are about to change around here... I've made a lot of bad deals, invested in stupid ideas, and pissed away more money than I could earn in a lifetime."

The walls were still standing, but the house seemed empty. He probably didn't offer us a drink because he couldn't even afford that. This man had lost everything—and that was why he looked like shit.

"The crows will descend and take everything away. Then the hounds will take the carcasses. My daughter won't be safe on her own. They'll come for her next...and do terrible things to her." He closed his eyes as if just saying the sentence was too much. He might have lost everything, but his love for his daughter was still alive. "The only way I can keep her safe is by marrying her to a strong man, a man who comes from a good foundation, a man that can protect her."

He'd described me perfectly—but that didn't mean I wanted her. "I'm not looking for a wife, Martin. Maybe you've gotten the wrong impression of me, but I'm not any different from the crows and hounds you described. I'm cruel—and I won't be any different toward her."

Martin turned to my father. "But you're both men of your word. If you promise me you won't hurt her, that'll you protect her, then I know you'll keep your promise. I'm giving you the thing you want the most—in exchange for what I want the most. It's a fair deal."

I felt my father's gaze on the side of my face, the burn of his eyes as they drilled through my flesh. All he wanted was Ramon's corpse—he didn't care what it cost to acquire it. But I didn't want to take on a pet, a nuisance.

"You said you never wanted to get married anyway," Father said. "So it's not like you're making a sacrifice."

"But I am making a sacrifice," I snapped. "I don't want to deal with an annoying brat. I don't want her living in my house, running her damn mouth, getting in my way." I knew avenging Mother was the most important things in our lives, but I hated what it had to cost. I turned back to Martin. "Why don't you take her and hide somewhere? Move to Iceland and start over."

"I can't." Martin inhaled a deep breath, but it sounded as if his lungs struggled to expand all the way, so he coughed into his hand, convulsing at the table.

Everything made sense in that moment. His sickly appearance...his pale skin.

He wiped his mouth with an old cloth that he kept inside his pocket. "I won't be around to protect her. I'm not sure what will claim my life—a bullet or cancer. But it'll be one or the other...and it'll be soon."

I almost pitied him—almost.

Father turned to me. "Martin, give us a moment."

I knew how the conversation would go before he even said a word. I watched Martin walk out of the room, and when he was gone, I spoke before my father could give one of his famous speeches. "I want Ramon dead as much as you do, Father. We will find him—one way or another. Our time is coming. Forcing me into this marriage will only speed up the process. Let's take our chances."

Instead of being angry, disappointment filled his eyes. "There's nothing your mother wouldn't have done for you—"

"I know—"

"Interrupt me, and I'll shoot you again."

My mouth shut automatically because I knew he would make good on his threat.

"I listened to you, and now, you'll listen to me. Your mother sacrificed everything for you and your sister. She gave birth to you, took care of you, put up with you when you were little brats. Now she needs us. Are you going to sit there like a selfish little pig when we have an opportunity to do the right thing?"

"I think Mother would want me to marry a nice girl and have lots of babies. It would be different if she were alive. I would do it in a heartbeat—but she's already dead. This doesn't change anything."

His eyes were so steady, it was disturbing. "It changes everything. You will do this, Maverick. Or I'll kill you."

I stared at my father as the numbness set in. Ever since my mother had been put into the ground, he'd become a different person. I'd expected him to recover slowly, to emerge gradually from the dark side of the moon and return to the brightness of the sun. But he was progressively slipping away, disappearing further and further into the unknown.

I still remembered the man I'd once looked up to, the man who wore his heart on his sleeve. He didn't have to tell us he loved us because he showed it with his smile, with his affection. But now that she was gone, he was gone too. He was just a shallow shell of who he used to be, someone plagued by regret, bloodlust, and terror. I wasn't his son anymore. I was just a tool in his box. I was just a means to an end. When Mother died, his love for us died too.

In that moment, I felt like I had nothing left to lose. "Fine...I'll do it."

2

ARWEN

My diaphragm tightened as I hit my last note. With my mouth wide open and my lungs screaming in pain, I filled the auditorium with my strong voice and brought the production to a close, seeing the curtain close in front of me as I finally ran out of breath.

The lights were bright, roses were thrown onto the stage, and I could see the audience rise to their feet as they gave a standing ovation. The adrenaline I received was more powerful than any other high I'd ever known, better than sex with any man. It was euphoric, dreamlike.

I watched the curtains close as time stood still. Ever since I was a little girl, this had been my dream.

To be an opera singer.

Now I was.

With the curtains closed, the symphony concluded. That only made the applause louder, the sound of whistling and cheers more audible. I stayed on the spot and enjoyed the moment a little longer, cherished the connection I felt with every stranger in the room. They could have spent their

Friday night doing anything else—but they chose to spend it with me.

DANTE CAME backstage with roses in his hands. He was tall, handsome, and had the cutest smile, and his eyes lit up as he looked at me. He came right up to me and kissed me. "You were amazing."

"Thank you…"

He presented the roses to me. "I could watch you sing every night."

"And I'd love to sing every night if my voice could handle it." There was already a vase sitting at my makeup station, so I set the roses inside and added some water.

"So how about I take you to dinner?"

"Singing for two hours does make me hungry."

"Perfect." His arm hooked around my waist, and he escorted me out of the theater, making this night even more magical.

I PULLED up to my childhood home and felt the presence of previous generations the second I stepped foot on the grounds. The house had always been large for three people, but now it felt too big for just one.

I entered the house and searched for my father, noticing how it seemed particularly dark. I carried a fresh arrangement of flowers and put them in a vase in the kitchen, just to lighten the place up. My mother used to be the same way, freshening up the house with flowers directly from the garden. She'd been gone a long time now, but I still carried on the tradition.

Father stepped into the kitchen, wearing jeans that were too baggy around his waist and a shirt that also seemed too loose. He was paler every time I saw him, sour like spoiled milk.

He kept telling me nothing was wrong—but now, I wasn't sure if I believed him.

"There's my princess." He walked up to me and kissed me on the head. "How was the show last night?"

"Full house with a standing ovation."

"Wow, that sounds amazing. This country can't get enough of that voice of yours."

"I don't know about that...but thank you."

He eyed the pink lilies in the vase, giving them just a glance before he turned back to me. "How are things with you?"

"Good. You know, just lots of work and lots of practice." I'd been meaning to introduce Dante to my father, but since he was the first man I would bring home, I was nervous about it. My father had always been protective of me, and I wasn't sure how he would feel about it. But then again, there probably wasn't a single man he would ever think was good enough for me. "What about you?"

"You know, nothing too exciting."

We moved to the dining table with a pitcher of lemonade and made small talk. I told him that the opera wanted to add a few more shows, but since I needed to preserve my voice, they would use my understudy. We talked about the weather, the football game, and other things that didn't really matter.

He started to cough harshly, pressing a napkin to his face as he heaved at the table.

"Daddy, are you alright?" I placed a hand on his shoulder, concerned that this cold wasn't going away. It only seemed to get worse with every passing week. "Are you sure the doctors said you're okay? You look worse every time I see you."

He wiped his mouth and chuckled. "Well, that's a nice thing to say."

"Come on, you know what I mean. You don't seem well… Is there something you aren't telling me?" Would my father keep something like that from me? Would he lie to my face and pretend everything was okay when it clearly wasn't?

His smile faded away as his eyes filled with the distinct gloss of melancholy. Like impending tears in a painting, his emotion was clear in the subtleties of his gaze. Sometimes the cliff face of despair was more obvious than the tears themselves. "I'm fine, princess. But there's something I need to tell you… You aren't going to be happy about it."

"Alright…"

"The money is gone. I can't pay my debts, I've screwed over a lot of people, and soon, men will be crawling all over this place and picking it apart piece by piece. I've pissed off some scary men…and they won't be happy."

I had both French and Italian blood, and I came from a line of wealthy aristocrats I was proud of. Our fortune was massive, and while I never asked for a penny more of it than what was in my trust, I'd assumed it would always be there when it was time to inherit it. "What…? What are you saying? We don't have any money?"

He shook his head. "No…not a euro."

Money wasn't important to me, but knowing it wasn't

there terrified me. Without my share of the trust, I couldn't afford my nice apartment, I couldn't afford to keep performing because it didn't pay enough. I couldn't afford food or clothes. "I don't understand... How did this happen?"

"It doesn't matter," he said with a sigh. "It doesn't change what's going to happen. Bottom line, we're broke. That means we're also in danger..."

I couldn't believe this was happening.

"I'm sorry, princess. I know you're disappointed in me... I'm disappointed too."

I wasn't anything at the moment. As long as we were both healthy, we could figure out a new plan. I would have to get a day job if I wanted to keep performing at night. I'd have to reconsider my career options now that I couldn't live off our wealth. It was devastating...but doable.

"There's only one way I can keep you safe...and you aren't going to like it."

"Keep me safe? I'll give up all my possessions and take them to the bank to pay our debts. Whatever it takes."

"No, not from the banks. I have worse enemies than the banks..."

I didn't ask because I didn't want to know.

"The only way you'll be protected is if you marry into another family, a powerful and rich one, one with enough credibility that they won't bother with you. You'll be unattainable."

"Well, this isn't the 1800s, Dad. Arranged marriages are absurd in this day and age."

"Maybe...but it's necessary."

So he was serious. "You aren't thinking of actually marrying me—"

"I've already found the perfect husband for you—Maverick DeVille."

I had no idea who that was. "Uh...not gonna happen."

"Arwen, I know this is hard, but this is about survival. We won't survive unless we do this. You have no idea what kind of men will be hunting me down."

"What about you? Why don't I just go with you?"

"Because you'll be on the run forever. You'll never have a normal life. You'll never be able to sing again. Maverick can keep you safe. He can keep the dogs away. I know you don't like this, but trust me, this is what—"

"I'm already seeing someone..."

"Well...I'm sorry."

"You're sorry?" Now that I realized that this was deadly serious, that my father really intended to marry me to some stranger, the terror was starting to suffocate me. "You're sorry that you're making me marry a guy I don't even know? Well, the answer is no. I refuse."

He bowed his head. "Princess—"

"Don't 'princess' me." I pushed my hands against the table and stood. "When I marry someone, it'll be for love. It'll be because I can't live without him. I'm not marrying some guy because I'm scared of your collectors."

"Arwen, you don't understand." He rose to his feet, moving much more slowly.

"I'm not listening to this." I started to walk off, refusing to entertain this nonsense.

"Arwen." His voice grew stronger. "You don't understand what you're up against."

I stopped in my tracks, the tears immediately burning to the surface.

"I won't survive this. And when I'm gone, there's nothing standing between you and death. Arwen, I don't want to say this to you...but these men won't just hurt you. They'll rape you...they'll torture you. I wish there were another way...but there's not. Maverick DeVille is the only way you'll live. So, we don't have a choice."

.

3

ARWEN

My apartment became my fortress for the next few days.

I dodged my father's calls even though I felt like shit for doing it.

I sat at the kitchen table with a bottle of red wine in front of me. It was one of those nights when I didn't bother with a glass. Getting my hit straight from the bottle was the only way to guarantee my satisfaction.

White candles were lit on the table before me, setting up a beautiful ambiance so I could practice my singing. A window that stretched from the floor to the ceiling was beside me so I could see Florence underneath me, the Catholic church just a few blocks over.

But I had no interest in singing.

My life had been turned upside down in a matter of seconds. All my freedom had been stripped away, all of my independence. Now my family was in such trouble that I had to marry some random guy.

Like that was ever going to happen.

As much as I loved my father, I was angry with him. How

did he ruin our livelihood? How did he destroy my inheritance? How did he get involved with such cruel men that my life was really that vulnerable?

How could he do this?

I'd already lost a mother. Now I would lose a father.

Dante knocked on the door.

"It's open." I rose to greet him, to greet the only person in my life who could offer any comfort.

He stepped through the door wearing a collared shirt and jeans. He had dirty-blond hair, bright eyes, and a handsome face that was borderline boyish. A hint of a smile was on his lips, and happiness shone in his eyes. But when he saw my expression, all of that joy faded away. "What's wrong?"

"Everything." My chest tightened because air was too painful for my lungs. My life had been so simple a week ago. I'd had a family fortune that would keep me and future generations wealthy until the time stopped, but now I was penniless. My father squandered everything we had—including his life.

"What are you talking about?"

I didn't cry because I refused to shed tears. The last time I'd sobbed my heart out was at my mother's funeral, and it hurt so much that I vowed never to do it again. Crying made me feel weak, made me feel useless. It didn't solve the problem, and it only made me pathetic. "My father just told me he lost everything...all of our wealth."

Dante was still as he stared at me, as if what I'd said was so ridiculous, he couldn't believe it. "What? How?"

"He didn't give me any specifics." And it didn't matter either. Whatever he pissed away our money on didn't matter anymore. Our bank accounts were empty, and our debtors would still come to collect.

"But your family is worth a fortune. How could he just spend it all?"

I shrugged. "I don't know...I really don't." I'd wanted Dante to come over tonight not for interrogation, but for comforting. But I had to tell him this horrific news, how our lives were about to change forever. "He said he was marrying me off to someone because it's the only way he can protect me..." I knew that would be the worst piece of news, the revelation that would affect us the most. Dante and I hadn't been together long, but the sparks were flying. It seemed like we could have a future together...if we were together long enough to experience it.

Dante's concern slowly stretched away, replaced by a stony look. As if it were a defense mechanism not to react, he kept his feelings bottled deep inside. That boyish charm was gone, and there was only devastation in its wake.

"He said a lot of dangerous men will hunt him down, and unless I want to run for the rest of my life, I don't have a choice. I guess this man is powerful enough that I'll be untouchable...at least, that's what he says."

"Who's the guy?"

I rolled my eyes. "It doesn't matter. I'm not marrying him."

"If you aren't marrying him, then what are you going to do?"

"I don't know... We'll run to France. I still have relatives there."

"Then isn't that the first place they'll look? Will your relatives be safe?" He was speaking reason, but I didn't want to hear any logic right now.

I grabbed the bottle from the table and took another drink.

Dante kept watching me with his pretty eyes. "Who is he?"

"Maverick DeVille...whoever the fuck that is."

Dante's eyes narrowed in recognition. "I recognize that name. His family owns a cheese business outside of Florence. It's been in their family since the days of kings."

"My father wants me to marry a guy who smells like cheese?" I asked incredulously, not the least bit impressed with his family wealth. "If he made wine, then at least he would be somewhat useful. But cheese?" I made a disgusted face. "This is not happening. And how does that make him powerful?"

Dante's eyes lowered as he considered the question. "A lot of wealthy families have ties to the underworld. Maybe he uses the business to launder his money. He's not the first one... Sounds like your father did the same."

Why did rich people waste their wealth trying to get richer in sleazy ways? "This is a nightmare. I keep thinking I'll wake up any second, but I never do." My hair was a mess because I'd been fisting it all night, making it frizzy because I kept yanking on it and spinning my fingers through the strands.

Dante didn't absorb the information quickly. He sighed quietly to himself then moved toward the large window, thinking about the load of turmoil I'd just dropped on him. Our relationship wouldn't survive what was coming. We couldn't run away together because we would get caught. And if we got caught...we would both die.

I refused to marry Maverick, but I had no other options.

None.

But I was more stubborn than a mule, inheriting a decisive attitude from my mother. I didn't take orders like a good soldier. I wanted to be the general, to call out the orders and watch lesser men obey me.

My father wanted me to sacrifice everything I believed in by marrying this stranger.

But I'd rather die...

4

MAVERICK

Bernadette had drifted off to sleep beside me. Her leg was tucked in between mine, and her palm was flattened against my hard stomach. Her parted lips rested against my hot skin, still wet from our kisses. Her breathing was slow and steady, implying she would sleep in such a state of peace that she may never leave.

But I wouldn't allow her to stay.

No one was allowed to stay.

My phone vibrated on the nightstand, and my father's name showed up on the screen.

It was difficult for me to see his name without feeling a rush of hatred. That man's gaze was focused so tightly on one goal, he forgot about all the objects in his peripheral vision—including me. I was just a tool at his disposal. I did his clean and dirty work and never expected a thank-you.

I certainly wouldn't get one now.

I left the bed and didn't bother being gentle. Her head fell to the pillow, and she sighed as her precious sleep was disturbed. Just to be obnoxious and get her to leave, I answered the phone. "Father." The name was nearly ironic coming from my lips. He hadn't felt like a father for a long time. "Caspian" seemed more appropriate at this point. I walked to the table near the window and lit a cigar. Looking out the window, I could see the lights contrast against the beautiful city. Lights were pointed directly at every cathedral, illuminating the beautiful history of his amazing place. Once the smoke started to smolder, I blew it out of my mouth.

"Martin will introduce you to Arwen tonight."

So, she had agreed to this arrangement? I hoped the woman had more class than to accept an arranged marriage. If she refused, I would have gotten out of the deal. Also, I would have respected her for it. But now it seemed like I was stuck. "Alright." My father really expected me to go through with this, to marry and subject myself to domestic torture even though it wouldn't change what had happened to my mother. I'd be considered selfish for refusing—but he was selfish for asking.

"He's taking you to the opera tonight."

Great...I was already going on a first date. I'd just fucked Bernadette thirty minutes ago, so my dick still smelled like her. But now I had to put on a suit and meet a woman I would never care for. She would have my name and my protection—but she would never have me. "Alright."

"Do you know how to say anything else besides *alright*?" he challenged.

I took another puff of my cigar and felt the rage boil in my blood. "Maybe if you said something interesting, I would."

MARTIN and I took our seats in the first row, but there was no sign of his daughter.

Maybe she'd had a change of heart.

If only.

Martin didn't look as sickly when he was dressed in a suit, but his pale skin was more noticeable when the stage lights hit him. "My daughter doesn't know about my condition... and I'd appreciate it if you didn't mention it to her."

I had no interest in family affairs. I gave a slight nod of acknowledgment. "Where is she?"

"You'll see her in a moment. She's the opera singer in the production tonight."

An opera singer? I imagined a large woman blowing her pipes so the entire auditorium could hear every single note of her monstrous voice. I'd never asked for her age or a description of her appearance. Regardless of how she looked, I would despise her all the same. But if she were considerably older than me...it would just be awkward.

Minutes later, the curtain rose and the symphony began.

Standing in the center in a tight black dress was a petite woman looking out to the crowd like she owned the auditorium. She hadn't moved her lips or made a sound, commanding the stage with her silence. White gloves reached her elbows, and the pearl necklace around her neck made her seem like royalty. With pink cheeks, lips painted the color of red roses, and thick brown hair that was pinned to the side, she looked like a porcelain doll. Her eyes were the most obvious because they were a startling blue, like the deepest ocean in the world. She didn't blink once as she absorbed the audience, fearless as a warrior, a soldier who used her voice as a weapon. Then she began to sing...and shatter glass with the power of her voice. Strong and controlled, she weaved a beautiful picture with just her words and the way she sang them. It was loud like a cannon breaking down the entrance to a fortress, but it was so uniquely stunning that it was hypnotizing.

It only took me seconds to recognize her...the woman from the portrait.

SHE FINISHED ON A HIGH NOTE, sucking in the souls of every person in the audience before the curtains came to a close. Roses were tossed on the stage, slipping from the hands of male admirers. The symphony pulled their bows away from their strings, and the silence that followed was almost depressing.

The audience rose to its feet and clapped loudly, echoing off the high, gold-plated ceilings. It seemed to last for five minutes straight before people finally filed to the exits, wearing their suits and ball gowns.

When Martin looked at me, fatherly pride radiated from his smile. "Amazing, isn't she?"

I hadn't clapped for her, and I continued to relax in my seat as everyone else dispersed.

"I know I'm asking you for the favor, but you couldn't do better than Arwen Greco."

I wouldn't insult the man with a sarcastic comment, so I remained silent. She was definitely beautiful. If I saw her in a bar, I would have bought her a drink. That voice would be amazing to listen to in bed. But no amount of beauty or talent could make me grateful for this marriage. She could give me beautiful children...but that wasn't relevant because I didn't want any.

Martin took me backstage, and after weaving through different members of the production, we approached Arwen from behind. She was sitting at her dressing table, the white bulbs sticking out of the mirror frame to give her the ultimate lighting. She pulled the ribbon and flower out of her hair, letting the thick strands fall across her shoulders and slender neck.

We stopped behind her, and that's when I recognized this vantage point. This was exactly where she'd been sitting when the photograph was taken, which was then turned into a portrait.

I felt as if I'd stepped back in time, to the moment I met her countenance for the first time.

She looked up and recognized her father in the mirror. Within seconds, her carefree expression faded into one of obvious dislike. Her eyes fell in disappointment, and her anger was seething. It was the same look I gave my father—so I recognized it right away.

She turned around on her stool and rose to her feet, her curves outlined in the skintight clothing that could barely stretch enough to allow her lungs to expand to make those incredible sounds. Her waistline was incredibly slender, so small my fingers could cup one side of her waist completely. Her petite stature didn't mask her womanly charm, especially her fuckable chest. "What are you doing here?" She ignored me completely and faced her father with enough fire that it seemed like she could breathe it out of her mouth like a dragon.

Martin remained calm despite his daughter's rage. "Arwen, I'd like you to meet Maverick-—"

It was the first time she looked at me, and she didn't look at me the way other women did. She wasn't the least bit attracted to me, impressed with my broad shoulders or the way I filled out my suit. My structured jawline had no effect on her at all. She was indifferent. "It's *not* nice to meet you. Disregard whatever my father told you. I'm not marrying you." She grabbed her purse then stormed past us and headed to the exit.

With a stony face, I turned back to Martin, realizing I'd made the wrong assumption. This woman despised this plan as much as I did, but instead of being relieved at the notion, I was concerned. Neither one of us wanted to participate in this vile arrangement proposed by our fathers, but if it didn't happen, my mother would never be avenged. My father would never find peace.

Martin sighed. "I'm sorry…she's a little stubborn."

"A little?"

He shrugged. "Gets it from her mother. She'll come around…eventually."

I didn't believe that for a second. "I'll try to talk to her."

Martin released a sarcastic chuckle. "Maybe you are used to making mountains move—but not this one."

SHE LEFT out of the back exit and took the stairs to the side-walk near the road.

I caught up with her, moving toward her as her heels clapped against the concrete path. She was still in the shadow of the theater, close to the statues of the two lions that protected the grounds of this historical landmark.

"Arwen."

She stilled at the sound of her name, jumping because she'd assumed she was alone when she ducked out of her secret passageway. She turned on her heel and looked at me with the same fierce expression as before, her purse hanging off her shoulder. Now she looked even angrier at my appearance. "I said I don't want to marry you—"

"And I want to marry you even less."

Finally, she shut her mouth, shocked that I was the first man who didn't want her. She pivoted the rest of her body and faced me, suspicion in her eyes.

"I have no interest in being a married man. There's no woman on this earth that could possibly keep my attention long enough. I like my life the way it is—working, drinking, and fucking. You may be beautiful, but not beautiful enough."

She never dropped her guard, but she didn't seem offended by the rude comment I'd just launched at her. Her hoop earrings shifted with every movement she made, reflecting the distant light from the street corner. It was a warm night, and a gleam of sweat formed down her cleavage. "Then why are you chasing me?"

"Because you're running." I spoke like a smartass because I wanted her to know exactly who I was. I was a fucking asshole—all the way through.

"Don't be a dick."

"I'm not being a dick. I *am* a dick."

She stepped closer to me, like she had a knife hidden somewhere in that skintight dress and she was looking for the perfect place to cut me. "Why did you agree to marry me? If you're as powerful as my father says, then no one can force you to do anything."

Only one man could. "It's my father's wish." When she was this close to me, I could smell her perfume, her hair spray, and the scent of the dusty curtains of the opera house all at the same time. I could even smell her confidence because it had a scent…of fresh flowers.

"It's my father's wish too, but you don't see me bending the knee like a pussy."

My eyes widened because I couldn't believe something so harsh came from such a pretty mouth. "You'll be bending the knee with your ass in the air every night if your father's enemies find you. They'll fuck you bloody then stab you in the gut until you bleed out and die, scared and alone. Then they'll hang you in the countryside until the police find your corpse, your eyes plucked out by the crows. I'm your only chance of survival."

She kept up her fearless stare, but her eyes showed a hint of doubt, like my vivid picture scared her on some level—as it should.

"You're too stupid to understand how dire your situation is. You literally have two options—life or death."

She continued to hold my gaze, not backing down or intimidated like most people. She was alone with me, her screams too far away to reach someone who could help her. But she didn't seem to care about the danger she was in. She didn't seem to understand the magnitude of her defeat.

"Then I choose death." She gave me a final look of dismissal before she turned around and walked off, her heels echoing against the concrete as she made her way further into the dark night.

5

ARWEN

<small>W</small>HAT WAS <small>I</small> GOING TO DO?

I couldn't marry him.

I wasn't naïve about my current position. Everything Maverick said was true. I had no options right now. I could either marry him or subject myself to the cruel torture of the men who wanted to punish my father.

I wasn't stupid.

I was just stubborn.

My life had been perfect before this happened. I loved my job, I loved the man in my bed, and I loved my independent existence in this luxurious apartment. But all of that disappeared with the snap of a finger.

Now I had to give it all up.

Maverick warned me about the men who would hurt me.

But what about him? Who was he?

Would he hurt me just the same?

I grabbed another bottle of wine from the cabinet and uncorked it, the room filling with the sound of the audible pop. I drank directly from the bottle once again, not wanting to hand-wash all the glasses sitting in the bottom of my sink.

A knock sounded on the door—but I wasn't expecting company.

Then it opened, even though it'd been locked just a moment ago. Maverick emerged into the entryway, wearing dark blue jeans and a black t-shirt. Last time I saw him, his frame had been hidden underneath a suit, but now his clothing showed muscular arms, thick veins, and narrow hips. When he spoke about his bachelor life, it didn't surprise me at all. He picked up ass on the town and fucked pussy until he wanted a different flavor. Why be with one woman when he could have them all?

But that didn't impress me. I'd been with men just like him before. Nothing special about him at all.

A knife was sitting on my table, so I grabbed it and gripped it in my hand, the blade pointed in his direction. "Didn't your mother teach you to knock?"

"Yes. But I was a terrible child." He walked farther into the room, making himself welcome when my hostility was unmistakable. He came right up to me and took the bottle from my hand. "Barsetti vineyards... You have good taste in wine." He helped himself to a drink then sat in one of the dark wooden chairs, resting the bottom of the bottle on his thigh while his fingers still grasped the neck.

I kept my grip on the knife even though he didn't seem hostile.

He took another drink and eyed the weapon in my hand. "Are you going to smear some butter across my abs?"

My fingers loosened at the mockery. "Get the fuck out of my apartment, or I'll stab this in your neck."

"Geez...you are not a lady at all."

"Did I say I was?"

He set the bottle on the table. "Your father made it seem that way. But I guess he was just trying to make a sale."

I was being compared to livestock—and I didn't appreciate that. "Get out."

"No." His long legs stretched out beneath him, his knees apart and his muscles obvious in the places where his jeans hugged his body. His shirt was tight across his chest because his pectoral muscles were thick enough to make a dent in his clothes. His skin was very tanned, like he didn't spend much time indoors—unless he was fucking. To every other woman in the world, he was a handsome and rich man.

But to me, he was just a bastard. "I said, get out."

"And I said no." He nodded to the other chair. "Take a seat."

"I'm not a dog."

"Never said you were...even though you're acting like a bitch."

With lightning speed, I slammed the knife down onto his thigh, intending to stab him as deep as I could.

He moved his leg out of the way then caught me so I wouldn't slam into the hardwood floor underneath his chair. "Be careful. Don't want you to hurt yourself." He took the knife out of my hand and started to help me up.

I pushed off him and straightened.

"You've got great speed but terrible aim. I can give you some pointers if you want."

"Sure." I crossed my arms. "How about we practice on you?"

A slow grin crept onto his face, the first one I'd seen him

make. "You're a pain in my ass, but at least you're entertaining. I'll give you that." He tossed the knife on the table. "You know why I'm here. You need to change your mind because we're running out of time. Make this easier on everyone and take advantage of your only option."

"I said I'd rather die."

"Then you must not understand what death means if you choose that."

"No, I understand perfectly."

"Alright..." He crossed his legs and rested one ankle on the opposite knee, getting comfortable in the wooden chair. "Then you must not understand how terrible it feels to be raped by a group of men. How painful it is to be a punching bag. And since you're so entertaining, they probably won't kill you...so your one way out won't be available to you. It sounds like I'm your only option. Never thought I'd have to work so hard to get a woman to marry me when I don't even want to marry her."

"I think the answer is pretty obvious—you're soft."

His smile disappeared immediately, like I'd provoked the beast within. "Trust me, I'm not soft."

"You're begging a woman who despises you to marry you. That's pretty pathetic, if you ask me."

"I'm negotiating a deal—a deal that needs to happen."

"To please your daddy?" I mocked. "I thought women were the ones with daddy issues..."

His gaze darkened once more, like I was poking at a wound that was festering. "My mother was kidnapped, raped, and beaten. Before my father and I could rescue her, they killed her. You wanna know how?" He tilted his head as he looked at me. "They hanged her. Your father came to mine and said he would give us the man who destroyed my family if I married you." He raised his hand and pointed it at me. "Why would I want to marry some annoying brat who doesn't understand her father is trying to save her life? Why would I want to marry someone so goddamn stubborn, she actually thinks she has another way out? Why would I want to marry a little girl who thinks she's some big, tough man? Trust me, the last thing I want to do is see you in a wedding dress and give you my name." He rose to his feet, towering over me the second he stood upright. "But I have a duty to my family—to my mother. If this is the price I have to pay, so be it." He stepped closer to me, his face coming near mine as he stared me down with pure loathing.

It was the first time my tongue felt too big for my mouth, when I knew I'd shoved my foot too far down my throat. I shouldn't pity this man, but I did—and I felt terrible for the insensitive comments I'd made. "I'm sorry about your mother...and the mean things I just said. I take it back."

"No such thing as takebacks." He stepped back, his presence still dwarfing everything in the room. "I need you to marry me because I have to avenge my mother. You need to marry me because no one will touch you as my wife. We need each other. So, stop prolonging it and just give in."

That was what anyone else would do...but I wasn't like everyone else. "You don't know me very well, but I'm not the kind of person that just gives up."

"Marrying me wouldn't be giving up. You would be choosing life, not death. If you run, you won't make it very far. If you stay, they'll find you even quicker. Taking my name will blanket you with invincibility. My family isn't a family you go to war with—especially not for a woman. You can keep your life, just with a few subtle changes." He grabbed the bottle and took another drink, his head turning and showing the prominent angle of his jawline. It was so sharp, it seemed to be carved out of glass. His chin was covered with a shadow of hair, just as it'd been a few nights ago. With classic dark looks and brown eyes almost the color of coffee, he was pretty on the outside...but dark within.

"I'm seeing someone."

"So? I'm seeing lots of someones." He turned back to me.

"I won't sleep with you."

"Is that supposed to bother me?" The corner of his mouth rose in a smile. "You think you're so beautiful that every man wants to fuck you? Sorry, sweetheart, but I've seen better."

I'd never met a man so cold and cruel. I didn't care if he found me beautiful or not, but he was so vicious, it was hard to believe. But at least he wouldn't force me to do anything I didn't want to do. "I've seen better too."

"I doubt that..."

I couldn't help but roll my eyes at his misplaced arrogance. "Will you hurt me?"

"Depends."

"Depends on what?" I demanded.

"If you piss me off. Just don't piss me off, and we won't have any problems."

"Well, don't piss me off, and I won't kill you in your sleep."

He chuckled like I was nothing but comical to him. "I always see what's going on—even with my eyes closed. Any other requests?"

"I want to live alone."

"No, that won't work. You'll have to live with me. The world will have to think you're really my wife. That means keeping your mistresses...or misters...discreet. I don't have to do the same thing because—"

"You're a pig?" I snapped.

"Something like that."

The more I got to know him, the less I liked. "I want to continue to sing at the opera. It's my life."

"Couldn't care less."

"I want to have children."

He opened his mouth to make a comment, but then he closed it again, as if he'd misunderstood what I said. "Wait... you mean you *don't* want to have children."

"No. I do want to have children."

"Well, I don't."

"Fine. Then I'll have them with someone else."

"But they'll be under my roof. I can't allow that."

"There's nothing you can do to control when I get pregnant or not. So, you can either be the father, or you don't have to be. Doesn't make a difference to me. But I will have a family one way or another. Not anytime soon...but someday."

With that dark countenance, he stared at me with a stony expression, like he was annoyed by the request but felt helpless to fight it. The situation was out of his control, and he knew it. No point in arguing about it. "Is that a yes, then?"

"A yes to what?"

"That you'll marry me."

Ever since I was a little girl, I'd imagined a much better proposal than this. For one, the guy would be someone I loved. And second, it wouldn't be under these horrific circumstances. Plus, the guy wouldn't be a huge pig.

He continued to watch me as he sat and waited for a confirmation.

I slowly lowered myself into the chair and grabbed the bottle of wine. "I don't know..." I brought it to my lips and took a deep drink, needing the sweetness of the fruit along with the booze to calm my beating heart.

With one arm resting on the table and an indifferent expression, he watched me. "You do know. You just don't want to do it."

I took another drink.

"Your father is trying to help you. Let him help you."

I nearly spat out the next sip of wine I took. "Help me? If he wanted to help me, he could have not spent our family fortune on god knows what. He could have avoided all these bad men he's talking about. If he really gave a damn about protecting me, he wouldn't have put us in such a vulnerable position. It's not just irresponsible...it's unforgivable."

Maverick stared at me with cold eyes, looking at me like I was a painting rather than a person. "You can be a brat and whine about the past, or you can move on. I suggest you move on...if you don't want to die."

"I'd rather be a brat than an asshole. This information dropped on my shoulders just a week ago, and I'm supposed to be over it?"

"You should have been over it the moment it happened. There's no point in living in the past. It doesn't matter that you used to be some rich little princess. Now you're piss-poor —unless you grab on to the only life raft you've got." He rested his fingers under his chin as he regarded me. "Life will always throw surprises your way. How you react to them is what defines you. Feeling sorry for yourself is one way to go... but it won't get you anywhere."

This man was heartless and lacked any ounce of empathy.

He didn't care about my story and what I'd endured. That indifference would carry on into our marriage, and I would be married to a man I didn't even like. We couldn't even be friends. "Have you always been this cold?"

He regarded me with the same expression, frozen down to his core. "You call it cold. I call it pragmatic." He rose to his feet and towered over me once more. "I'm going to assume your answer is yes." He turned to the door to leave.

"Wait."

He turned around.

"I don't even know you..." I knew nothing about him other than his name. I had no idea what he did for a living, what his favorite color was, what he believed in. We'd shared a bottle of wine and had a conversation, but I knew him even less than I did before.

After another cold look, he turned back to the door. "Does it matter?"

6

MAVERICK

MARTIN OPENED THE DOOR HIMSELF BECAUSE HE COULDN'T afford his servants anymore. Dressed in pajamas and a t-shirt, he seemed almost too tired to get out of bed anymore. His illness was obvious to anyone who looked hard enough. It was a mystery that Arwen didn't notice with her fierce intelligence.

Or maybe she just didn't want to see it.

I didn't wait for an invitation before I stepped into his entryway. "I talked her into it."

Martin straightened his back, forcing his weak muscles to work to give him proper stature. He stilled once he heard what I said, and his right eyebrow arched so high in puzzlement. "Are we talking about the same woman?"

I was impressed he could crack a joke in his condition. Mortality didn't faze him like it did most people. With melancholy in their eyes and defeat in their limbs, they gave up before the fight was even over. "Yes."

"Then hats off to you." He mimicked a bow. "You really

should marry her...since you're the only one that can talk some sense into her. You must be persuasive."

Just bossy.

"Thank you for doing that. And of course, I'll uphold my end of the bargain."

I wouldn't marry her unless he did. "You better. Because if you don't, I won't be kind to your daughter."

His smile dropped with the threat. He could make a joke about anything, even in his condition, but a threat to his little girl, he couldn't brush off as easily. "I'm a man of my word. I assume you're a man of yours?"

"Always."

"Then be good to her. I know she has a bit of an attitude, but the best mares always do. They know what they are worth and don't settle for less. They're beautiful, but they aren't afraid to get their hands dirty. My daughter's qualities are also her flaws. When you get to know her, you'll see just how magnificent she really is. This might be a means to an end for now...but maybe you'll come to love her in time."

Love wasn't in my vocabulary. "I won't hurt her. You have my word."

He released the breath from his lungs, coughing with the effort.

I watched this sick man and actually pitied Arwen. She'd already lost her family inheritance, but soon she would be an orphan as well...and she had no idea. "You need to tell her the truth."

He wiped his mouth with a handkerchief. "I know."

"You need to do it soon. It's cruel to keep her in the dark when she could be spending time with you."

"That's the very reason I haven't told her. After what I did, she has every right to be angry with me. Betraying her the way I have and then dropping the truth on her shoulders... would be so conflicting. It would take away her right to be angry. She deserves to be angry."

"You can't change the past, Martin. But you can savor every minute of the present."

"I know..." His eyes dipped down as he continued to breathe through the ache in his chest.

"How much time do you have?" Every time I saw him, he seemed to look worse and worse. His skin was becoming pastier, his breathing was even louder, and the bloodshot look to his eyes deepened.

"It's not a science," he said. "But a couple weeks. Truth be told, I hope I die before the shit hits the fan. Would much rather die in my sleep than be butchered with a knife. And if I'm really lucky, I'll even be buried next to my wife before any of that happens."

It was hard to believe he was capable of such stupidity when he seemed to truly love his family. "Why did you do it?" Men gambled with their fortunes and their lives when they were stupid or greedy—usually both. But this man seemed a little wiser than the rest.

He shrugged. "Just like you said, we shouldn't live in the past..."

Fair enough. "Then we should have the wedding next week. I'm assuming you'd like to give her away."

"Yes..." His eyes glossed over as he imagined it. "I know this isn't the wedding she wants. You aren't the man she wants. But it's still the best protection I can give her. Maybe one day, she'll thank me for it..."

Maybe.

"Even if things change in time, you must stay married to her. Even when the dust settles, you can't go back on your commitment. Do we understand each other?"

That meant she would be my wife until the day I died. I'd see her face every day, see her resentment as the years turned into decades. Maybe we would have children, and perhaps that familial bond would bring us closer together. Or maybe we would hate each other until our dying breath. "Give my family our revenge, and consider it done."

WITH A CIGAR IN MY MOUTH, I made the call I'd been dreading.

I wasn't afraid. I just loathed every moment I spent talking to this man.

Father answered. "Is it done?" He'd told me what would happen if I failed. A second bullet wound would be in my shoulder, next to where he shot me the first time. Sometimes I felt like a servant rather than a son.

"Yes."

A congratulation never came. Not even a thank-you. I fulfilled his expectations; I deserved no reward. In his eyes, everything he asked for was so basic, only an idiot wouldn't be able to do it. "Then marry the bitch so we can start preparing."

"It'll have to be a public wedding with guests if we want people to take it seriously."

"How is that my problem?"

"You'll have to be there." It was ridiculous I had to ask my father to come to my wedding—even if it was fake.

He practically growled on the phone. "Fine. How long does the bastard have to live?"

"Weeks."

"Then we need to hurry this up before he croaks. I need to know exactly where Ramon will be—so I can choke him with my bare hands."

7

ARWEN

I LAY IN BED WITH DANTE BESIDE ME.

Sex used to be good, used to be hot and sweaty. But now that everything had changed, the fire that used to burn our skin had gone out. I was stressed about the future, so my libido had faded. Dante must have felt the same way, because his desire wasn't as potent.

With my face on his chest, I lay beside him, thinking about how much my life would change. I tried to convince myself it wouldn't be that different. I would live with Maverick, but I wouldn't be in a relationship with him. I could still work, still sleep with Dante. It was just a change of scenery.

That's all.

At least, that's what I kept telling myself.

I watched Dante stare at the wall, his thoughts a million miles away. He was naked in this bed with me, but his thoughts weren't on sex. They weren't even on me. "What are you thinking about?" I propped my head on my hand and ran my fingers down his frame.

He didn't shift his gaze to me. "I don't see how this is going to work."

"What?"

"Us."

My heart stopped beating. "Why wouldn't it?"

"You know why." Bitterness was heavy in his tone.

"Nothing will change. It's just a display."

"Maverick DeVille is still a powerful guy. I don't want to cross him."

"He said I could sleep with whoever I want—and he could do the same. It's just a show, Dante."

"Still...you're another man's wife."

"Maybe...but I don't belong to him." I continued to run my fingers down his chest, feeling the grooves of his abs. "Nothing has to change, so I don't know why you have a problem with it. Our relationship can be the same as it was before."

He finally turned his gaze to me. "But I can never marry you."

My fingers stopped moving when I finally understood. He didn't have a problem with my marriage. He didn't have a problem with Maverick. But he had a problem not making me his.

"It'll always be a secret. It'll be an affair. We'll have to keep our relationship private, which means no public dinners, no family gatherings...just sex. That's fine for the meantime, but it won't last forever."

I hadn't thought that far down the road. I just assumed I could have everything I wanted—on the side. But now I realized how unfair it would be to the other person. They would always be second best. The gravity of what I was giving up really hit me. I would never truly fall in love because a man would never love a married woman.

It hit me hard.

A knock sounded on the door.

My eyes turned to the open bedroom door through which I could see the entryway. It was almost nine in the evening, far too late for a random visitor. I slipped out of the sheets and pulled on my robe.

Before I could even leave the bedroom, Maverick walked inside my apartment.

"Do you mind?" I stepped out of the bedroom and shut the door behind me, hiding Dante's naked body from view.

Maverick's eyes glanced at the door, catching a glimpse of my lover before he turned back to me. With no apology, he pulled an envelope from his back pocket and tossed it on the kitchen table. In a t-shirt and jeans, he once again looked fit, having the kind of body that seemed bulletproof. "No. You can finish when I'm done."

Was this how our lives would be? He would barge into my room whenever he felt like it? "Knock. I'm warning you."

"Or what?" He challenged me, not the least bit afraid of my ferocity.

"This." I slapped my palm across his face.

He barely turned with the hit, and even when my hand collided with his face, he didn't seem angry. If anything, he seemed amused.

"Don't barge into my apartment again."

"Otherwise, you'll slap me again? Fine. I don't mind it."

Jesus, he was infuriating.

Maverick behaved like nothing was odd, like it wasn't awkward that I had a man in my bed at that very moment, behind a closed door. He acted like I hadn't just slapped him, like he had every right to step on my property as if he owned it. "Talk to your father. You've dragged it out long enough."

This man hardly knew me, but he spoke to me like my family affairs were his concern. "Don't tell me what to do."

"Believe it or not, I'm helping you."

"I find that hard to believe..."

He cast his cold gaze on me then gestured to the envelope he'd dropped on the table. "We're getting married on Saturday. Buy a dress—something nice. There will be lots of people there."

"What people?" I asked, as if that was the most important sentence he said.

"My people." He dismissed the conversation by turning away.

I grabbed the envelope and spotted all the cash stuffed inside, tens of thousands of euros. "What the hell is this?" I threw it at his back. "I don't need your money."

He turned back around, annoyance spreading into his hard gaze. "Now isn't the time to be proud."

"I'm not being proud. I just don't need your money."

"You need a nice dress."

"And I will get myself something."

"With what money?" he demanded. "You literally own nothing now. Everything in this apartment will be seized in weeks. You'll be my wife, which means I don't want you to look like a slob. Make yourself look decent so our wedding day will be a little less terrible—and a little more believable."

"Wow...I despise you." Every conversation we had was worse than the last. Soon, he would be just down the hall and a million times more annoying. I would have to spend whatever money he gave me because I didn't have any other choice.

He opened the door and turned back to look at me like I was nothing to him. The room could have been completely empty given the indifference written on his face. "A wolf doesn't care if the sheep likes him. All he cares about is eating the sheep—and you're my sheep."

ONCE I ACCEPTED MY FATE, I showed up at my father's house.

I'd been bitter about everything and everyone. I was disappointed in my father for destroying our wealth. I was angry that a bastard like Maverick would be my husband. I was hurt that Dante didn't want to be with me for the long term.

Every single cornerstone of my foundation had been ripped from underneath me.

I wouldn't be surprised if I lost my job at the opera for no reason at all.

That was the kind of luck I'd been having.

My father was quiet as he sat across from me, but he wore a small smile like he was happy to see me.

We hadn't said a word to each other. I let myself into the house because there were no servants to do it anymore. Now I sat across from him at the table, hardly able to look him in the eye because I was so upset with him.

How could he do this to us?

My father gave me the floor, providing me the opportunity to speak first.

But I had nothing to say. I was only here because I

couldn't avoid him forever. On Saturday, I would marry a man I hated...and I didn't want to do that alone. My father was all I had. It would be strange if he weren't there...even if it wasn't the happiest day of my life. "The wedding is on Saturday." I finally forced the words out, accepted the terrible truth. "I bought a dress..." I'd always thought shopping for my wedding dress would be a beautiful affair. My friends and I would drink champagne and eat chocolate-covered strawberries as I tried on every beautiful designer dress. But instead, I walked to the closest shop to my apartment and picked the dress I liked the best.

I didn't even try it on.

To make it worse, I handed over the cash Maverick gave me.

And signed my soul over to the wolf.

"That's nice," Father said. "I'm sure it'll look stunning on you. But you could wear jeans and a t-shirt, and you'd still be the most beautiful bride."

Flattery wouldn't work on me—even if he meant it. "I'm still so angry all of this is happening. The only reason I'm marrying Maverick is because he foretold my fate if I rejected him. He's a cold and irritating man, but I'll admit he's better than the alternative..." At least the man wouldn't rape me. At least he wouldn't hurt me...I think. I tried to stab him and he didn't retaliate, so I was probably safe. "But I'm losing Dante...I'm losing my freedom...I'm losing everything." My hands rested on the table, and I finally lifted my gaze to meet my father's eyes. "I'm so angry with you for all of this. This is entirely your fault." It was a cruel thing to say, but I didn't care. "I'll never marry a man I love because of you. I'll never have the family I want because of you. You've given me to

Maverick to protect me, but if you really wanted to protect me, you should have made different choices." It pained me to speak to my father this way, but the situation was crushing my chest.

My father looked at the table as he gathered his bearings. After a deep sigh, his shoulders sagged, and he looked at me again. "You're absolutely right, princess. It is my fault. I shouldn't have been so arrogant. I should have been more cautious. Now I'm leaving you with nothing... It's terrible."

Hearing his admission didn't make me feel better. It didn't give me any satisfaction to be validated. The pain was exactly the same.

"I'd do anything to take it all back..."

I knew he would. My father had made a mistake, but he wasn't evil. "I know..."

"I wish this wasn't happening. I wish you weren't marrying a man you don't love. I wish for a lot of things...but wishing doesn't get you anywhere."

No, it doesn't.

"But Maverick is a powerful and honorable man. He'll keep you safe."

I wasn't looking for a man for security. I was looking for a man for love.

He saw the disappointment in my eyes. "I understand if you hate me."

His actions were enough to garner that reaction, but I couldn't bring myself to feel that way. "I don't. I never could."

His hand moved on top of mine, like that meant the world to him. "Princess, there's something I have to tell you..."

My eyes lifted to meet his. So much terrible news had been dumped on my plate already. Could there possibly be more? Why couldn't the universe give me a break? Why couldn't life be fair...the way it used to be.

He squeezed my hand as he took a deep breath, wincing like his words were painful before they even came out of his mouth. "I have cancer...and I don't have much time."

8

ARWEN

Just when I hit rock bottom, I fell a little further.

Now everything was numb, ice-cold, and fragile. My fingers were frozen to the bone, my heart stopped beating with the same vitality, and my legs weren't strong enough to hold my weight. The idea of marrying Maverick killed me... but this was so much worse.

So much fucking worse.

I couldn't show my tears, not when my father was the one who had to die. My job was to be there for him, to help him through this difficult time and make him as comfortable as possible. He only had weeks left, so I put aside our issues and was the daughter he needed.

I stayed at the house, cooked all of his meals, watched TV with him, and helped him with anything he needed. We watched his favorite movies, looked through old photographs, and tried to remember happier times.

But when he was asleep, I let myself cry.

Let myself sob into my darkest night.

I sat at the dining table with a cup of hot tea in front of

me, watching my tears splash into the steam. When my father left this world, I would be the last of my line, the last of my kind. With no brothers or sisters, I was completely alone in this world.

Maverick would be my only family...by name.

I still didn't want to marry him, but my father's demise made me understand how alone I truly was. He wouldn't be there for advice. He wouldn't be there for guidance. I would be completely on my own—with vultures following me.

Perhaps Maverick was my savior after all.

My phone rang, and Dante's name popped up on the screen.

I answered it, tears audible in my voice. "Hey…"

He sighed when he heard my sadness. "I'm so sorry…"

"I know." I wiped my tears with the back of my thumb and willed myself to stop crying. Crying wouldn't change anything—but I was so devastated.

"Is there anything I can do?" His deep voice came over the line, carrying the weight of his sorrow.

"No. But I'm going to stay with him until…it's time."

"I understand. If there's anything I can do, just let me know."

"Okay…" I stared into the hot tea in front of me, wishing this were a nightmare I would wake up from. I wished this were just a bump in the road. But the harsh truth was my reality...and it was unbearable.

"So, it's still happening on Saturday?"

"Yeah…" I really had no choice now. There was no going back...but there was nowhere for me to go. Dante certainly couldn't keep me safe. He would be murdered with me. "You told me how you feel about it, so I understand if you want to stop seeing each other..." The last thing I needed was to lose the only comfort that I had, but I knew he couldn't fix this for me. No one could.

"No...I'm not ready for that."

"Good." I needed a man to get through the dark nights I was about to face. "Me neither."

———

WHEN I OPENED the large mahogany door, I looked up into the face of Maverick.

With his dark hair, coffee-colored eyes, and the shadow of hair along his structured jawline, he stared at me with that stony expression, as if he had no grasp of what a smile was. The bright sunshine of the summer behind him brought a darkness over the front of his body, matching the dark blazer he wore and his dark jeans.

I kept my hold on the door handle and stared him down, matching his stoniness with my coldness.

He shifted his weight slightly, straightening his shoulders as if I were an opponent rather than his fiancée. Whenever this man was near me, his posture was always hostile. Maybe that was directed me—or maybe that was just how he was.

"Are you going to invite me inside, or should I just barge in like usual?"

My hand gripped the handle because I was tempted to slam the door in his face. "Why are you here?"

"Your father told me you were looking after him." Instead of waiting for my invitation, he stepped inside and pushed past me.

I stared at the landscape through the door, the red geraniums blooming out of the pots along the walkway. It was a beautiful day, but I was in no mood to enjoy it. I shut the door and turned around. "You knew the entire time." I crossed my arms over my chest.

"Yes." At over six feet, he made a dent in the enormous room. His muscled shoulders stretched out his blazer, and his veined hands peeked out from the ends of his sleeves. His jeans were snug, showing the definition of his muscular legs in some places. He was a beautiful man with a beautiful body —but an ugly soul.

"And you didn't think you should mention that to me?"

"It's not my place."

Hearing that my father was dying was horrifying—no matter who said it. "He's sleeping right now."

"I'm not here for him."

"I hope you aren't here for me—because I'm not yours yet."

The corner of his mouth rose in a smile, like he found my attitude comical rather than intimidating. Sometimes, Dante was put off by my brashness, and other men didn't appreciate it either. They said I was too much to handle. But Maverick clearly thought I was a joke. "I have something for you." He pulled out a small black box from his pocket then stepped toward me. He snapped open the top and revealed a princess cut diamond ring with diamonds along the band. The diamonds were clearly flawless—because they were practically blinding.

I stared it, shocked that Maverick was capable of picking out something so elegant and stunning. It was exactly the ring I'd always dreamed of getting. It was so simple but so sleek. I yanked my gaze away from the brilliant diamonds and looked at him again.

"You like it."

"I never said that."

He pulled the ring out of the box then grabbed my left hand. "You don't need to." In something akin to a romantic gesture, he slipped the ring onto my finger. Except it wasn't romantic at all, just a formality. He kept his eyes glued to mine as he released my hand.

It was a perfect fit. Just to be stubborn, I didn't raise my hand to admire it, even though I would the second he was gone.

He slipped the box back into his pocket. "I'll be back tomorrow. Your father and I have business to discuss."

"I'll let you know how he's feeling. He's getting worse by the day."

"Then we can't put this off."

"Thanks for being so sensitive about it..."

He stepped closer to me and lowered his voice. "I'm sorry your father is dying. But my mother is already dead. Don't expect me to cry a river for you."

"At least you still have a parent..." This man was evil—right down to the bone.

His eyes shifted back and forth slightly as he looked into mine. He could command soldiers with that look, lead countries with that stare. He was strong and ominous, every bit as unnerving as my father described. If there had to be someone looking out for me, it seemed like there was no one better. "The grass is always greener on the other side..."

9

MAVERICK

Father reached the door first. "He better not die today, not before he gives me what I want." He pounded his fist against the door, slamming his knuckles into the wood like he was there to capture the fortress rather than just pay a visit.

If Arwen thought I had no compassion, wait until she met my father. "We'll get what we want. But let's be delicate. The man only has weeks, if not days, to live." I didn't have much pity for Martin—but I did pity his daughter.

My father turned on me like I'd insulted him. "Was anyone delicate when your mother died?"

God, I knew he'd say that.

When his cheeks started to puff, I knew he was losing his temper. "Was anyone sensitive to my wife being raped—"

"We're here and he's alive. So let's just get what we came for. No need to make a scene."

"What did I say about interrupting me?" He grabbed me by the neck and started to choke me.

I threw my arm down and pushed him off. "Enough."

"If I had my gun, I'd shoot you."

You'd think I'd be numb to his cruelty, but it was like a fresh wound every single time. "Then how would you hold up your end of the deal? I'm the one marrying her—like you asked."

His eyes narrowed. "I'd shoot to wound, not to kill."

"Be careful. Because I shoot to kill—every time."

My father stared at me coldly, his eyes turning aggressive at my threat. He'd been getting away with his offensive behavior for almost a year. His wife died, so he thought it entitled him to be the world's biggest ass.

I could only tolerate so much.

Arwen opened the door. "That's quite a loud knock you've got there..."

My father looked her over, unimpressed, and then stepped inside the house without issuing any kind of greeting.

She watched him move past her before she cocked an eyebrow and looked at me. "I see where you get it from."

That was the worst insult she'd ever given me. I followed my father inside. "How is he?"

My father wouldn't even tolerate the simple question. "It doesn't matter how he is. He made a promise to us, and he will keep it...unless he wants his daughter to end up like your mother." He walked off and headed to the dining room in the rear of the house.

She watched him go, her eyebrow staying raised like she couldn't believe his audacity. She turned her gaze back to me, still in shock at his rudeness.

"Now I don't seem so bad, huh?" I smiled even though I didn't feel an ounce of joy inside my body, then headed to the entryway.

"I'll get my father..." Arwen took the stairs.

When I passed the kitchen, I took a bottle of wine and a few glasses then joined my father.

He was huffing and puffing like a wolf about to blow the house down. He looked straight ahead and drummed his fingers against the table, so noticeably anxious that he made all the figures in the paintings anxious too.

I poured the wine and pushed the glass toward him.

He ignored it.

Maybe it was an evil thought to have, but sometimes I wished my father had died and my mother had lived.

At least she was a good person.

Martin walked into the room moments later, looking worse than the last time I saw him. He walked a little slower, breathed a little heavier, and it seemed like his skin was about to drip off his face.

Arwen pulled out the chair for him and helped him sit down. Concern was in her blue eyes, and she looked after her father with obvious love. She wasn't the fierce woman with an attitude that could bite. Now she'd been reduced to her rawest emotions, her fears. Her father was going to die, and there was nothing she could do to help him...but she tried anyway. "How about some water?" She rubbed his shoulder as she looked down at him.

"Yes, thank you."

She walked off, her diamond ring shining on her left hand.

My eyes went to the portrait of her on the wall. Now I noticed a distinct contrast between the painting and her physical appearance. That ring made all the difference in the world, and without her wearing it, she seemed like a changed person. It subdued her somehow, like a bridle on a horse.

My father cut right to the chase. "Ramon. Where is he going to be and when?"

Martin turned to me. "It's nice to see you again, Maverick. I'm sorry I missed your visit yesterday—and thank you for the beautiful ring—"

"I asked you a question." My father took over the conversation once more, ignoring anything else that wasn't relevant to what he wanted. He was focused on one task only—to the detriment of everyone around him. "I don't give a shit about your pleasantries. We made a deal, and you need to spit it out now or I'll—"

"You'll what?" Arwen stepped into the room, carrying the glass of water in her hands. She wore a dark blue dress that complemented her dark hair. Pearls encircled her neck, and her hair was pulled to the side, hanging down in a braid. The glass hit the table with a noticeable thud as she faced off against my father.

Arwen didn't understand boundaries.

But neither did my father.

Martin cleared his throat. "Princess—"

She raised her voice a little louder, matching my father's rage with her own. "Or you'll *what*?"

My father stared her down, clearly surprised someone was standing their ground against him. He didn't know if he should get up and slap her in the face or just smash her head into the wall.

"Asshole, this is how deals work." She placed her hand on her hip. "You get your shit when both sides of the deal are completed. I haven't married your son, and you haven't gotten your information. That means we don't owe you a damn thing yet. So shut your mouth, or I'll shove this bottle of wine so far up your tight ass—"

My father launched to his feet. "You—"

"No." I was in between them, so I rose to my feet and blocked them from each other. My father wouldn't hesitate to hit a woman. I'd seen him do it before—just not to my mother. I grabbed his arm and kept him steady so he wouldn't launch himself at Arwen. "We both need something here. So let's all shut our mouths and focus on what matters. Father, sit." I turned to Arwen. "Be silent."

She grabbed the water again, still staring at my father with obvious threat. She wasn't scared of him like most people—because she had no idea what kind of crimes he could commit. She walked to the other side of the table, her heels clapping against the floor as she moved. Then she set the glass of water in front of her father.

I guided my father back down into the chair. "Let's get what we need and leave."

When my father's attention was directed to the reason we came here, he calmed slightly. He lowered himself to his chair, his back rigid with tension, and finally stared at Martin.

I looked at Arwen. "Leave us."

Her attitude fired up again. "So you can berate my father—"

I stood instantly, my next words exploding like a command. "Don't make me ask you again." I was ordering her out of the room for her own good, because I couldn't protect her from my father if she provoked him too much.

"I'm not a dog," she said calmly. "I don't obey orders—"

"Princess." Her father patted her hand. "Let the men talk. I'm getting hungry, so how about you start dinner?"

She was too smart to believe anything he said. She stared at me with those narrowed eyes and tightly pressed lips, like this was far from over. Then she turned on her heel and slowly left the room, her hips shaking from left to right because of her feminine curves. When she was finally gone, so was the tension.

My father got right down to business. "I need all the details, Martin. Since you're almost dead, time is of the essence."

WHEN MY FATHER got what he wanted, he stormed out of the house and left me behind.

He didn't need me anymore. He disappeared just as abruptly as he'd arrived. He didn't say another word, didn't even give his condolences to Martin about his illness.

I drank my glass of wine until it was empty.

Martin stared at the painting of his daughter for a long time like I wasn't even in the room. "When I lost my wife, I was the same way. Bitter about everything. I didn't lose her in such a violent way, so I can't even begin to imagine how your father feels."

"Don't make excuses for him."

"I'm not." He turned his gaze back to me. "He marches in here like the villain—but he's trying to be the hero."

He was no hero in my eyes.

"I'd like you to take this painting with you. I noticed you admiring it last time you were here."

Admiring was a generous word. "It doesn't match the other pieces in this room."

"It's not supposed to. I just loved it so much that I thought it belonged there. Everything in this house will be stripped away—I'd like that to survive. Take it with you."

I had no interest in taking a portrait of a woman I didn't even like. "Martin, I'm marrying your daughter because I have to—not because I want to." There was no affection for her in my heart. I was barely impressed by her beauty—even though most men found her stunning. I'd been around beautiful women for so long that they all looked the same.

"Maybe...but your children might want this painting someday."

I hated imagining a reality where Arwen was pregnant with my child—a little brat inside her. They'd piss and shit all over the place.

Martin slowly rose then made his way to my end of the table. "That ring you gave her really is beautiful. Just between you and me, I think she's already gotten attached to it."

I could tell she liked it the second I gave it to her. Her reaction was very sudden and short, lasting only the length of a blink of an eye. But I caught it. She still didn't like me, but she obviously liked pretty things. "Will we see you on Saturday?"

"I'll make it to Saturday—but not much further." He spoke of his death so pragmatically, like he wasn't the least bit scared.

"You seem oddly calm about this whole thing."

"Well, I lost my wife five years ago. When you lose the love of your life, nothing is ever the same. You always feel a little lost. Thankfully, I had Arwen to give me some joy through these years, but truth be told, I'm looking forward to being reunited with her."

It was beautiful...in a sad way.

"I wish I could be around longer to see the incredible things my daughter will accomplish...but I'll watch her from upstairs." He placed his hand on my shoulder and gave me a gentle squeeze. "I know you'll take care of my little girl. If you'll defend her from your father, you'll defend her from anyone. Goodnight." He dropped his hand and left the room. A moment later, his steps were audible on the stairs.

Arwen came back to the dining room and cleared the glasses. "My father went to bed?"

"I think so."

She still had an edge to her, obviously not quickly forgetting the conversation with my father. "Has he always been like that?"

"No."

"Really?" She held the wine bottle by the neck, cocking an eyebrow like she didn't believe that for a second. "He just woke up one morning and decided to be an asshole?"

"No," I said calmly. "My mother died, so he decided to be an asshole."

Her rage dimmed slightly, like a fading star on the other side of the galaxy. "My father went through a phase after my mother was gone...not quite as bad, though. He was more sad than angry."

Yes, but her mother hadn't been tortured. "I'm not his biggest fan either, so you aren't alone."

"He doesn't treat you like that, does he?"

I wasn't going to complain about my father issues to her. I didn't even know her. "Your father said he's looking forward to the wedding. I was thinking maybe afterward we could make him comfortable at the hospital."

"As nice as that sounds, we can't afford it. Our accounts are empty."

"I'd pay for it, obviously."

She gripped the neck of the bottle tighter, her pride wanting her to refuse the offer. But her concern for her father's well-being was clearly more important. She even managed a kind response. "Thank you..." Her voice trembled as she said the words, like she was barely holding on to her composure. When she launched an attack against my father, she didn't skip a beat. But now that she was alone, emotion overwhelmed her. Her bottom lip trembled, but just for a second.

I looked away, not wanting to deal with her tears. "It's no problem." I pushed my glass toward her and admired the way her ring reflected every single point of light that emitted from the chandelier. "Need anything else before Saturday?" I wanted to change the subject, to steer away from the heartbreak on her mind.

"No..." She grabbed the bottle and brought it to her lips.

I watched her tilt her head back and down the contents, her throat shifting as the liquid descended to her belly. Her neck was so slender, her waist so petite. It was hard to believe such an incredible voice could come from a woman so tiny.

She wiped her mouth with the back of her hand. "What's going to happen on Saturday?"

"We're getting married...or have you forgotten?"

She flashed me a look of menace, the evidence of her tears gone. "After the wedding. Are we going on a honeymoon? Because I need to stay with my father."

I wasn't whisking this woman off to an exotic location to fuck her brains out. I did that every night with an endless line of beautiful women. "No."

"Are you expecting to consummate the marriage?"

The corner of my mouth rose in a smile. "If you want to fuck me, just tell me. Don't beat around the bush—"

"Go fuck yourself." She stormed off into the kitchen, bringing the glasses and bottle with her.

I couldn't wipe off my smirk as I followed her into the other room. "The answer to your question is no. There will be somebody in my bed—but it won't be you." I leaned against the counter and watched her set the glasses at the bottom of the sink, drops of red wine still visible at the bottom of the bowls.

"Thank god." She washed the dishes then dried them with a linen cloth. "Where will we live?"

"I live on the property where our family business is. It's about twenty minutes outside of Florence."

"Does it smell like cheese all the time?"

I crossed my arms over my chest. "Odd question —but no."

When the glasses were dry, she placed them in the cabinet with the glass doors. "After meeting your father, I don't find you quite as irritating...despite that sex comment."

"Yeah...he always makes me look good."

"I need to drive into Florence for practice and my shows. So I'll need a car."

"Done."

She dried her hands on the towel then examined me, her eyes filled with endless thoughts. "How is this going to work?

We just live our lives however we wish, but we live under the same roof?"

"You have a better idea?" I didn't care what she did on her own time. I didn't even care if I never saw her. All I needed to know was she was safe—to uphold my promise. We didn't have to share a single meal together or even talk. But for public events, she would have to be the woman on my arm.

"Do I bring my lovers back to the house?"

It was hard to imagine strange men coming to my property. I didn't care that they were fucking my wife. But I didn't want them snooping around. "I'd prefer if you went to their place. I'm not thrilled about the idea of random men staying at my estate."

"Fine. Will you wear a wedding ring?"

The question was absurd. "No."

"So, I have to wear one, but you don't?"

"It's different."

"You mean, it's sexist?" she countered.

"Actually, yes. I'll get one for the ceremony, but after that, I'll never wear it. It's not uncommon to see a man without a wedding ring. In fact, it's more common." I turned my head back to her and studied her steely gaze. "You want me to wear one?"

"Not at all. Just curious."

"Any other questions?" I didn't have any rules laid out because it was unnecessary. This was a total sham. All we had to do was pretend once in a while.

"Is there anything you expect out of me?"

I didn't have any expectations at all. "I already told you my life is about working, drinking, and fucking. Don't get in the way of that, and we won't have any problems. It's that simple." I pushed off the counter and righted myself. "I'll see you Saturday."

———————

SHE GLIDED her palm over my abs and slowly moved it up to my chest, worshiping the fitness of my body. Her nails slightly clawed at my skin before she made her way down to my happy trail once more. Naked and with perfect, firm tits, she was another notch on my bedpost. "So, you're getting married tomorrow?"

"Yes." With one hand behind my head, I stared at the high ceiling and the original moldings that were present when this estate was built hundreds of years ago. It'd been renovated, but some of the classic touches remained.

"She doesn't mind sharing her fiancé with another woman?"

I wasn't her fiancé. "No."

Her hand moved down to my soft dick, wanting to get me hard again so I could make her come.

I was spent for the night.

She pouted at my resistance. "Come on...fuck me." She gently massaged my balls.

My dread for the following day disappeared as she forced my dick to harden. I would take her on all fours, so I could stare at that fine ass as I pounded her until she buckled underneath me.

"There he is..." She pressed her face into my lap and started to suck.

I closed my eyes and enjoyed it, listening to the loud

sucking noises her lips made as she tried to get the whole thing in her mouth.

My phone started to ring on the nightstand. I glanced at the screen even though I intended to ignore it, and I saw my sister's name on the screen. There was no woman in the world who could get me to ignore that phone call.

I pushed her off me and took the call, walking to the window with the phone pressed to my ear. "Lily, will you be there tomorrow?" When I stood at the open window, I looked across the lit grounds to the iron gates that separated my property from the public.

Her silence was her answer.

I stared at the darkness of the night and felt the disappointment in my chest. "How are you?"

"I don't know... About the same." She sighed into the phone, like it was pressed right against her ear as she lay in bed. "I take three steps forward but two steps back."

"At least you're making some progress."

"But not enough progress..."

This wedding was a hoax, but it was the only wedding I would ever have. I wanted my sister to be there, the only person in my family I actually liked. But Mother's death and Father's ludicrous behavior pushed her to the edge...and now she was too far gone. "I understand." I couldn't push her if she wasn't ready.

"I'm sorry I won't be there..."

"Me too."

"Who's the girl?"

"Her name is Arwen. She's an opera singer."

"She sounds accomplished... Do you like her?" Distant tears were audible in her voice, probably pained that she couldn't give me the answer I wanted. But she had to work on herself right now. Nothing else was important.

She had an attitude that rivaled a stallion. Her mouth could unleash insults faster than bullets left a gun. She wasn't afraid to slap me when I deserved it—and even stab me if I deserved it. "She's fine."

"She's fine?" Lily knew I was marrying Arwen because I was being coerced into doing it, but she still found my response comical. "Is she pretty?"

She had an hourglass figure and a lovely face to match. Even if she didn't have such an incredible voice, she could probably charm the crowd on looks alone. Men tossed roses on the stage every night, not because of her pipes, but because of her tits. "She's fine."

Lily chuckled, and since it was so rare, it was beautiful. "I guess I'll see for myself...eventually."

"When you're feeling better, we'll get lunch." I tried to keep her positive because that was essential to her recovery. I was the only coach she had because Father seemed indifferent to her illness. To him, she was just a brat looking for attention, but since I experienced the same heartache, I actually had some compassion.

"Maybe," she said, her voice escaping as a whisper. "How's Father?"

"We don't have to talk about him."

"We're both thinking about him."

He was the monster who didn't live in a dark cave. He walked directly in the sunlight, stomping everything in his path. "He's the same."

"Do you think he'll come back when he kills Ramon?"

He was too far gone at this point. Killing Ramon wouldn't

suddenly make him human again. It would just cross off an item on his list—then he would never have anything else to work toward. "I doubt it."

"Yeah...me too. What does he think of Arwen?"

Just like with everyone else, he didn't give a damn about her. "I don't think he thinks anything."

"I feel bad for her. Her new father-in-law is the devil."

I didn't respect Martin for the quandary he put himself in, but I did admire his parenting approach. He was affectionate and loving toward his daughter—and even to me.

"How does she feel about all of this?"

"She's dreading it as much as I am. She has her own life—I have mine. We'll just be two strangers under one roof."

"I guess that's not so bad."

When we ran out of things to talk about, we sat in mutual silence, listening to each other breathe. I leaned against the wall and kept my gaze out the window, remembering how different my life used to be before Mother was taken. We were a family—all four of us. Now we were all in separate places—mentally and physically.

"I'll let you go, Mav. Good luck tomorrow."

"Thanks. I'll see you soon." I hung up and kept my gaze out the window, hating my father even more than I had before. He still had two members of his family left, but once Mom was gone, he wanted nothing to do with us. He failed to realize how much his daughter needed him...how much she was drowning. So I had to step up—because she had no one else.

10

ARWEN

I STOOD IN FRONT OF THE MIRROR AND LOOKED AT MYSELF IN MY wedding dress, seeing a reality I'd never imagined in my wildest dreams. The designer gown was perfect, so elegantly designed and fitted to my dimensions perfectly. Any bride would be happy to wear it.

But it meant nothing to me.

The only item I possessed that mattered was the diamond necklace around my neck, a gift given to me by my mother. Her own mother gave it to her when she turned eighteen, so it'd been in the family for generations.

In just a few moments, I would walk out of this room and see the three hundred wedding guests Maverick and his father had invited. Some of them were aristocratic members of society, so of course, I knew them. Others were their family members who would soon be my family members.

But mostly, they were strangers.

My father was dressed in a gray suit and tie, looking well despite his frailty. He approached me from behind, a smile on his face as he admired me in my wedding dress. "Wow." His hands moved to both of my arms, and he gave me a gentle squeeze. "Maverick is gonna fall in love with you."

Not a chance. "Thank you, Daddy." I had my hair in loose curls, letting the long strands stretch down my shoulders. I'd applied my makeup exactly as I did at the opera, pumping my lashes with mascara and giving my eyes a smoky look with the eyeliner. My lips were painted a tint of pink, a rosy color that wasn't overbearing. I was marrying this man because I had to—and I wanted to look like myself.

He continued to look at me in the reflection in the mirror. "I know this isn't how you imagined your wedding day. Your mother isn't here, and your fiancé isn't the man you wanted. But I think Maverick is a good man...and you might become fond of him."

I couldn't imagine feeling anything for him besides annoyance. Every word that came out of his mouth was an insult. He had no regard for anyone's feelings and always blurted out the first thing that came to mind.

He watched my eyes fall. "He's a man of his word. And in a world like this, that's so rare. He promised me he would never hurt you. He promised me he would take care of you. I believe him. That says a lot about his character."

That didn't mean he was bearable.

"He's successful...and you must have noticed that he's handsome."

I didn't notice at all. "Daddy, I know you're trying to make me feel better, but it's okay. I'm doing this to survive. I'm doing this so I can still have the life I want—with a few sacrifices. Maverick and I had a conversation, and we found a way to live our lives separately but also together." I turned around and looked at him. "No, it's not what I want...but it could be worse."

———

It was a dream wedding.

White chairs on a perfectly manicured lawn as the Tuscan sun shone overhead. Pink and white flower petals were sprinkled on the ground, and the three hundred guests rose to their feet as my father walked me down the aisle.

My father kept his body strong as he guided me forward, refusing to let anyone know he was struggling to live every second of every hour. He smiled despite his pain, happy to be a witness to my wedding—even if it wasn't a fairy tale.

The harp music played as I made my way forward, approaching the man waiting for me at the end. In a black suit and tie, he watched me come toward him, his brown eyes unblinking as he studied me. His expression was stony like always, but he allowed a hint of affection to enter his gaze. Everyone would notice if the groom hated his new bride, so he adopted a lie to match the story.

When he allowed his aggression to fade away, he was actually handsome to me. With the sun on his tanned skin and the shadow shaved from his chin, he looked like a man who could have been in my fantasies. He was tall, fit, and he carried himself like a man with pride.

But his soul didn't match his looks—and he was vile.

I made it the rest of the way, wanting this moment to pass so we could move on and forget about it. The only positive memory I would have of this day was walking with my father. I knew it was probably the last time we would ever be together like this, when he would be healthy enough to get out of bed. He would no longer be the man to take care of me—because he was now handing the responsibility to the man waiting for me.

When we reached Maverick, my father kissed me on the cheek. "I love you, princess."

"I love you too, Daddy." I hugged him, and I let the embrace linger for a long time. I should have pulled away sooner, but I didn't want to. It was the last time I would get the chance to hug him in the sunlight.

My father patted me on the back, understanding the emotions that were swirling around inside me. He was the one to pull away first, because he knew I would never move otherwise.

I walked the rest of the way and looked at Maverick, doing my best to control my trembling lip. Marrying this man wasn't nearly as bad as losing my father, and in that very moment, I felt like I was living with his ghost. I knew this moment would be a memory all too soon.

Maverick watched me, dropping his artificial look of affection as he stared at my trembling lip. His eyes fell as he looked at me, and in that instant, there seemed to be a hint of compassion. He did the unexpected and wrapped his powerful arms around my waist and pulled me to his chest, making my head turn the other way so I would have a moment of privacy.

The crowd aww'd at this gesture, assuming Maverick loved his new bride so much that he couldn't keep his hands off her.

But I knew he was just giving me a moment to say goodbye to my father, to swallow the sorrow at the loss. That made me hate him a little less, made me wonder if he did have a soul under that intimidating façade. My father seemed certain Maverick would take care of me...and maybe he was right.

Maverick gave me as much time as he could before he stepped back.

It was enough for me to breathe a few times, to steady my bottom lip, to keep my eyes dry and my makeup intact. It was a momentary reprieve from the unbearable reality of my world. I'd lost everything—and now I would lose the most important thing to me.

Maverick faced me, his eyes glued to my expression so hard he didn't even blink. He didn't stare at me like he was in love with me, but he stared at me like he could look at me forever.

The priest performed the ceremony, asking us to repeat lines when necessary.

In a daze, I did my part.

Maverick spoke with a powerful voice, fooling the audience into thinking he actually wanted me to be his wife.

I hadn't even considered the last part of the ceremony, the moment we would become husband and wife and share our first kiss. Now the moment loomed over both of us, the first contact we would share with our lips.

And it would be the last.

Maverick moved toward me again, his arms sliding around my waist as his neck bent down so his mouth could meet mine. He squeezed me against him as his mouth descended, landing on my lips with the softness of a cloud.

I kept up the act by wrapping my arms around his neck

and letting my lips brush against his. His mouth was softer than I'd expected.

The kiss only lasted a couple of seconds, and it occurred in the midst of clapping and cheering. Maverick didn't just peck me on the lips and pull away. He made it seem real, moving his lips against mine like he wanted to kiss me. His lips gently tugged on mine, every touch purposeful. A warm breath escaped his lips and filtered across my skin, smelling like mint and scotch mixed together. The taste was distinctly manly in a way I couldn't describe.

For a moment, I forgot I was kissing Maverick.

Because I actually liked it.

GUESTS DRANK their champagne and ate the slices of cake that were passed around. A rustic Italian feast had just been devoured for dinner, so everyone enjoyed themselves like they were at a five-star resort.

Maverick and I moved to the center of the clearing where we would have our first dance. One of his arms hugged the small of my back while he gripped my other hand. Placing our joined hands against his chest, he started to guide me on the dance floor as the classical music played.

We didn't say a word to each other as we danced, everyone watching us like we were a couple in love.

Maverick was in his element, taking the lead and guiding me like he had with so many other women. He knew how to dance, how to sway to the music without looking awkward. He was confident no matter what he did—even dancing with his bride.

He lifted my arm and spun me around before he brought me back into his chest, his head tilted down toward mine. His cheek rested against my temple so we wouldn't have to hold eye contact throughout the song.

The sun had set, so the lights strung across the property shone a little brighter. Candles glowed on the tables. The centerpieces were filled with white lilies and pink roses. Whoever Maverick hired to design this wedding did a fabulous job—too bad it meant nothing to either of us.

With all the strangers surrounding me, I felt alone. That forged a surprising alliance with Maverick. When my father was gone, he was all I would have left. It made me feel a little closer to him, made me feel less isolated. "Thank you for what you did earlier..." He'd come to my rescue so I wouldn't sob at the altar, break my father's heart with my tears. Without a euro to my name, I thought I would have to stay home and watch my father die in pain in his bed. But Maverick said he would give my father everything he needed to give him some dignity for his final days. He knew I was on the verge of tears, but he didn't make me feel worse about it.

"I understand this is hard for you." He turned his head and looked me in the eye. It was the first time we'd ever been this close together, our eyes locked on each other. His eyes provided a perfect reflection of the bistro lights hung across the property, acting as a mirror. Like warm coffee on a winter day, his eyes were the most gorgeous shade of brown.

I hadn't noticed the depth of their beauty before.

With confidence, he held my gaze like this moment wasn't unbearable. When he didn't spit out insults, he was actually pleasant. It was strange to think this man was now my husband, that I would wear his last name for the rest of my life. We were joined together, husband and wife.

I could feel his black ring against my fingertips, the thick band he would only wear for the evening. It wasn't a traditional ring, not made of gold like most. But it suited him well...even though he would never wear it.

"My father speaks highly of you."

"Not sure why." He continued to guide me across the floor, carefully maneuvering my long dress and not stepping on it.

"He said you keep your promises...and that's rare these days."

"That doesn't mean I deserve a good reputation. I'm not a good man, and I don't pretend to be. I'm too much like my father and not enough like my mother."

"Well, he thinks otherwise."

"He doesn't know me well enough."

"Or maybe you just don't know how to take a compliment."

His eyes narrowed on my face as his hand squeezed mine a little harder. "I don't want to insult my wife on our wedding day, so I suggest you choose your words carefully."

I smiled. "That's romantic..."

"I'm not a romantic guy."

"Yeah, I've noticed."

He turned his gaze away and kept dancing. He seemed to tune me out, like I wasn't even there.

"Why do you have such a poor opinion of yourself?"

"I don't. I just understand what I am."

"And why are you a bad man?"

"Do we need to have this conversation now?"

"Something else you want to talk about?" I countered.

"We could not talk at all." His eyes scanned the people around us, hardly giving me any attention.

"Alright…" Just when I thought I could connect with him, he pushed me away.

He danced with me in silence, preferring the palpable tension to conversation.

"When the night is over, where will we go?"

"Inside. I had my men gather your things from your apartment. You can go back tomorrow and pick up whatever else you need. The banks will seize it soon, so I suggest you grab what's important."

When the night was over, the mansion looming over us would be my new home. "And my father?"

"He has a room made up for him. We'll take him to the hospital tomorrow."

Maverick may be my husband, but he didn't have to take care of my father. He didn't have to spend any money on him. But he seemed to shoulder the responsibility without argument. "Thank you. It means a lot to me." If Maverick were more like his father, he would dump my father on the lawn and not think about him twice. The man did possess compassion; he just tried to brush it off like it was nothing.

He didn't look at me, ignoring my gratitude.

It didn't matter what kind of peace offering I made, Maverick never took the bait. Even if he had the chance to connect with me, he didn't want to. He was determined to be as distant with me as possible, to not even allow friendship to blossom.

The song finally concluded, the torture coming to an end.

Maverick dropped his arm from my waist, like he couldn't wait for the opportunity to walk away.

Then everyone clanked their forks against their glasses, the tradition that enticed the bride and groom to share a kiss.

Maverick hid his annoyance as he turned back to me, knowing we would have to share a few more kisses before the night was over. His arm moved back around my waist, and he pulled me into him again.

We couldn't connect through conversation or friendship. We were charged the exact same way, our attitudes clashing together like two bolts of electricity. We would never see eye to eye on anything.

But there was chemistry when we touched—however faint it was.

He lowered his mouth to mine and kissed me again, his full lips taking mine like last time. With the same precision, he took my mouth and made it his. His hand squeezed the back of my dress as he pulled me closer, making all the guests clap eagerly.

My hand pressed against his torso and felt the hardness of his body through his clothes. My fingers flinched when I came into contact with the hard wall, surprised by his unnatural strength. My hand slowly softened as I got used to his ripped physique, my breath filling his mouth as an unexpected jolt of desire fluttered through my body.

He pulled away and looked me in the eyes for a moment, like he knew exactly what I experienced when I touched him. But instead of making a smartass comment, he kept his thoughts to himself.

11

MAVERICK

The servants worked outside to clear the tables, silverware, and endless decorations that stretched across the property.

My maid took Arwen and her father to their rooms so I could go to the third floor and retire to my bedroom. I hadn't expected the wedding to last for so long, but once people had wine in their bellies, they turned chatty and lingered.

I would have liked to have a woman in my bed tonight, but it was too late now and I was too tired. I stripped off my tie and draped it over the back of the armchair then let my jacket fall off my shoulders. My fingers popped open every single button until the collared shirt fell down my arms. My watch came next.

A knock sounded on my bedroom door.

I turned around to face the entryway, unsure why Abigail would disturb me at this hour. There was nothing so important that she needed to bother me right this moment. "Come in."

The door cracked and then revealed Arwen, still in her wedding dress. With a sweetheart neckline and sleeves of lace, her dress was elegant but also formfitting. It highlighted her many curves, her plump tits, and narrow waist. Her hair was thicker than I'd ever seen it before, and she looked ready for a performance at the opera. Every person who watched her walk down the aisle thought she was stunning.

She must have followed me to my bedroom because Abigail wouldn't have brought her here without my permission. We'd shared several kisses throughout the night, and I suspected that was why she was here now. She hated me, but not enough to ignore the chemistry between us.

She stepped inside and shut the door behind her.

I'd never intended to pursue a physical relationship with her, but if she wanted to fuck, I wouldn't say no.

A man didn't say no to easy pussy.

She walked up to me, her blue eyes so damn bright. Her emotions were easy to read because she had the most hypnotic expression. She had men in her bed because she could get any man she wanted. With those full lips and nice tits, her admirers probably jerked off to her every night.

My hand slid into her hair, and I kissed her. My lips felt hers, but this time, it wasn't for show. My fingers found her slender neck, and I caressed the skin as I cradled her head and deepened the kiss, thinking about how I wanted to fuck her. She probably had a nice ass—but those tits were gorgeous.

She pressed her hands against my hard chest and pulled away. "That's not why I came here..." She licked her lips and dropped her gaze, like she was embarrassed she'd misled me.

I wasn't embarrassed I'd made the wrong assumption. I

was annoyed I wasn't getting sex tonight. "Then why are you here? Don't barge into my room like that."

"I knocked…"

"Then don't come to my door again. I'm not in the mood to talk. If you want to fuck, take off your clothes and get on the bed. If you came here for a chat, get the fuck out. I've already done enough for you. I don't need to put up with this shit."

She stilled in front of me as if she couldn't believe my outburst. "My father is asleep, and I can't find Abigail." She turned around and showed me the back of her wedding dress. "I can't get this off by myself, so I thought you could help me. But since that doesn't fit into your two categories, I'll just go. I'd rather sleep in this thing instead." She marched to the door, her head held high with rage.

I didn't feel bad for my outburst, but I did feel bad that she would have to sleep in that stiff gown on her wedding night. A woman never struggled to get her dress off on her wedding night…because her husband would always happily remove it.

I was her husband now. "Get back in here."

She stopped in the doorway and slowly looked at me over her shoulder. Normally, she would march off, but any extra time in that skintight dress was probably unbearable.

"Now." With my bare feet hitting the hardwood floor, I stepped closer to her. My bedroom was nice and cool, a break from the heat outside. I could feel the cool air brush over my bare skin.

She stared at me for another moment before she returned to me, her dress dragging along the floor because she must have slipped off her heels in her bedroom. She walked up to me, glanced at my hard chest, and then turned around.

I stared at the thirty-six buttons and sighed. She never would have been able to get this off without me, not even with a pair of scissors or a knife. My hand moved under her neck and gently pulled the hair away, a waft of her perfume hitting my nose. My fingers started at the top, and I unbuttoned the very first one, seeing the dress give just a smidge with the release. My fingers kept going, undoing one after another.

She was silent as she waited for me to finish, not interested in making conversation after my outburst.

I kept working, the fabric slowly coming apart and revealing more of her bare skin. Her straight spine was flanked by two sets of muscles, her fair skin unblemished and beautiful. There wasn't even a freckle in sight. She was completely smooth, untouched. I stared at her back as I went lower and lower, moving to the top of her ass. I couldn't see the top of her underwear yet, but if I kept going, I eventually would.

When the back of her dress was loose, she gripped the front and kept it pinned to her chest. "Thank you." She didn't give me another look as she headed to my bedroom door and walked out.

I stared out the open door even though she was long gone. Now my slacks were tight and uncomfortable because of the enormous bulge right in the front. I could feel the pulse in my dick as desire ran through my veins. Something about that gorgeous skin made me white-hot. The sight of the outline of her tits, the way her spine curved so deep at the base, the way her skin erupted in bumps as the cool air brushed against it...it all aroused me.

THE NEXT MORNING, I sat at the kitchen table and drank my coffee while I went through emails and notes on my phone. The newspaper sat beside me, but unfortunately, I didn't usually have time to read it.

My father's name popped up on the screen as the phone rang.

Well, there went my morning.

"Morning."

My father never issued a greeting. Even hello was too much for him. "Is he going to die soon?"

What a lovely question first thing in the morning. "Odd question."

"My sources tell me he doesn't have much time. He hasn't paid his debts and delivered what he promised. The guys are going to move in any day. For his sake, I hope he's dead soon. I'd rather die on a morphine drip than with a blade in my stomach."

I didn't share most of my father's opinions, but I agreed with him on that front.

"If he's got some time left, I suggest you slip him something so he can go with some dignity." He hung up.

I lowered the phone from my ear and considered what my father had just advised. Arwen wouldn't want me to kill him prematurely, but she didn't understand how terrible it would be if he didn't die naturally. Those men would make the last few hours of his life unbearable. If we did it soon, we could bury him next to his wife, and the men would move on.

Arwen entered the room, led by Abigail.

"Would you like some breakfast, Mrs. DeVille?" Abigail grabbed the pot of coffee and poured it into the empty mug on the table.

Mrs. DeVille. Fuck, I had a wife.

"Yes, thank you," Arwen answered. "But please call me Arwen..."

Good.

Abigail finished pouring the coffee then headed to the kitchen. "Breakfast will be ready in just a moment."

Arwen eyed me but didn't sit down.

I stared at her with my phone in my hand, knowing we were both thinking about the same thing. I would have taken her to bed last night if she'd wanted me to.

"Can I join you, or will you scream at me?"

Alright, I deserved that. "Yes, you may stay."

She pulled out the chair and sat down. She cupped the mug with both hands and brought it to her lips, taking a deep drink like she needed the caffeine to fully wake up. New makeup was on her face, and her hair was still wavy from the night before. It was the first time we'd sat together to share a meal, and it was the first time I'd noticed just how beautiful her complexion was, how her fair skin complemented those blue eyes so perfectly. She took another sip then lowered the cup to the saucer.

I was grateful she hadn't walked in until after my father hung up on me. The conversation would have brought her to tears. I set my phone on the table and looked at her, noting the slight bags under her eyes because she clearly didn't sleep well in her new home. But the exhaustion didn't take away her beauty. Nothing could compete with those vibrant eyes.

"When my father wakes up, I'm going to admit him to the hospital..." It seemed like she was testing the waters, to see if I was still going to support his treatment—and his death.

"Do you need any help?"

"No, I don't think so. I'll be at the hospital with him until...it happens." Right on cue, her bottom lip started to tremble, and her eyes glossed over with moisture.

I didn't deal well with emotion—probably because I didn't have any. But I didn't want to be a dick and tell her to leave and shed her tears somewhere else. "When my mother was taken, I wanted to get her back. I hoped she would be returned to us and we could be a family again. But at the same time...I hoped she was dead. I didn't need to know the details to understand how much she was suffering. Death would finally give her freedom. So when I heard that she had died...I was relieved. No one could hurt her anymore."

Arwen blinked her tears away and lifted her gaze to look at me.

"Just think of it that way. All the suffering will be over... and he'll be free."

12

ARWEN

My father was more comfortable at the hospital. With Maverick's money, he got a large private room with a nice view and a big-screen TV. It was quiet, so he got to relax and take a lot of naps. Now that we were at the end of this horrible journey, his strength was slipping away and he was exhausted no matter how much he slept.

But at least he was comfortable.

Days passed, and he wouldn't last much longer.

When my father was asleep, Dante stopped by for a visit. I moved into his chest and held on to him as I cried quietly, being careful not to wake my father.

Dante's hand smoothed over the back of my hair, and he pressed a kiss to my forehead. "I'm so sorry…"

My wedding ring was so heavy on my hand that I never got used to it, so I was always aware of the commitment I'd made to Maverick. But it was all just a meaningless display so I could kiss this man without feeling guilty.

Dante tilted my head back and kissed me on the lips. "Is there anything I can do?"

I pressed my lips tightly together and shook my head. "No...it'll happen any minute now."

He continued to run his fingers through my hair, consoling me in whatever way he could manage. After he held me by the door for thirty minutes, we took a seat together at my father's bedside.

Dante held my hand, his fingers careful not to touch the large diamond on my ring finger. "How was the wedding?"

I shrugged. "Beautiful...but meaningless."

"Is Maverick good to you?"

He was spiteful and aggressive, but not a complete dick. He had his good moments...and his bad moments. But it could be worse. He could be violent with me. When I'd said I wasn't there to sleep with him, he could have easily forced me...but he didn't. He didn't control my life, giving me the freedom to do what I wanted, when I wanted. I didn't have any right to complain. "Yes."

Dante continued to hold my hand, our fingers interlocked on his thigh. There was nothing he could say to ease the pain of losing my father, of becoming some man's wife. All we had was this moment together—and nothing more. We just sat together, holding on to our connection before it was extinguished forever.

Minutes later, Maverick walked inside. He was dressed in his usual attire, dark jeans and a t-shirt. A watch sat on his wrist, but that was the only jewelry he wore. His boots thudded against the floor as he made his entrance. His gaze went to Dante first, probably recognizing him from my bedroom a few weeks ago.

Dante lifted his head and looked at him, tensing noticeably when he guessed exactly who he was.

Maverick stared at him for several seconds, noting the way our hands were joined together at my father's bedside. He looked at me next then moved to the other side of the bed. He slipped his hands into his pockets and watched my father.

I felt the tension rise in the room as the two men breathed the same air. Dante disliked Maverick because he was married to me, but his hatred didn't run deeper since he was good to me. But it was still awkward for him, especially when I continued to wear my beautiful diamond ring.

Maverick seemed indifferent to him, but I knew him enough to understand he didn't like Dante in the room. His mood was dark, his silence profound. His displeasure was so obvious that I was certain Dante could feel it.

I knew it would only get worse until one of them left. "Dante, I'll call you later."

Dante pulled his hand away and didn't argue. "Alright." He leaned in and kissed me on the mouth.

I kissed him back.

Then he left the room.

Maverick continued to stand there, watching my father sleep.

I stared at him, waiting for him to have some kind of an outburst.

But he didn't say anything about Dante. "He's not looking too good."

"He doesn't have much time left."

He looked at the monitor and checked his vitals like he understood what any of it meant. "Is there anything I can do for you?"

"You've already done enough for me, Maverick." He paid for my father to stay in the hospital, and for a room like this, it was probably ten thousand euros every single day. It was a generous offer, regardless of how rich he was.

"I wouldn't have asked if I didn't mean it." He finally turned his gaze toward me, watching me, his powerful shoulders straight. He filled out his clothes well, all the muscles pulling the fabric in just the right ways. I'd seen him shirtless once before—and the man was ripped. I'd love to watch water drip down all the grooves of his abs before it made it into his happy trail. He looked just as hard as he'd felt against my fingertips.

"I know. But you've already been so generous."

Compliments bounced off this man like air particles. They never broke the skin and penetrated deep inside him. He was incapable of accepting anything positive and always responded cynically. "Dante doesn't care that you're married?"

It was an odd question—and very sexist. "Do your ladies care that you're married?"

His espresso-colored eyes took me in without blinking.

"Our relationship won't last. Since he can't marry me, he doesn't want to be my lover for the rest of our lives. He wants a wife and a family someday...and I can't give that to him." I wasn't necessarily in love with Dante, but I could see it going somewhere. We'd only met a few months ago. Maybe if we had more time, things would be different. It was a lost opportunity, but I didn't resent Maverick for that. He was just as unhappy about this marriage as I was. There was only one person to blame—but he was about to die. "I suspect that will always be a challenge for me. Men don't want to be a secret."

"That's exactly what they want. They want to be your lover—no strings attached."

"Maybe in the beginning..." Every time I tried to have a fling, it always turned into something more. Even when I didn't want to see them again, they wanted to take me out to dinner. Sex always led to a relationship.

"Then you must be good in bed."

I imagined he probably was too. "As a matter of fact..."

A ghost of a smile crept onto his lips, a glimpse of his human side. Whenever he softened, his eyes turned from black coffee to a warm cappuccino. He was much more handsome that way, when he didn't look like he wanted to kill someone. "That makes two of us."

I rolled my eyes.

"You can say it, but I can't?"

"I was graceful about it. You're blunt."

"And that's the difference between a man and a woman."

I crossed my legs and leaned back against the couch, wearing a pink sundress with my mother's necklace. Summer was upon us, and the days were growing warmer. I loved the Tuscan heat, but I wouldn't be able to enjoy it this summer... not when my father was gone.

He continued to watch me, studying my expression. "What are you thinking?"

My eyes shifted back to him. "Does it matter?"

"Your tone changed. I could see it in your eyes."

"Well...every few minutes, I'm reminded where I am... what I've lost." My eyes moved back to my father. "It's hard to forget."

Maverick walked around the bed and joined me on the couch. He took a seat, his heavy weight making a much bigger dent in the cushions than Dante did. Dante was just as tall as Maverick, but Maverick had at least an extra thirty pounds of muscle. He was lean but strong like a horse. His knee touched mine as we sat together.

"You don't have to stay with me... I'm sure you have stuff to do." I didn't know exactly what he did for a living. I didn't even know how his family had ties to the underworld. Truth be told, I really knew nothing about him. I didn't know about his finances, where anything was in the house, and if he had a swimming pool.

Maverick didn't move. "I'll stay...for a little while."

EVEN THOUGH I knew it was coming, I was still devastated.

I cried myself ugly, my face was swollen from the sobs, and my eyes bloodshot red. I convulsed because the sobs racked my body. The tremors made my fingers and toes numb. He passed away in his sleep, pain-free on a morphine drip, but knowing he wasn't here anymore still killed my soul.

Now I was in my bedroom, sitting on the couch and staring at the stone-cold fireplace. Tears streaked down my cheeks and splashed onto my black dress. My fingers rested against my lips, feeling the drops as they made their way to my chin.

A knock sounded on the door.

I stayed quiet.

The door opened, and Maverick walked inside. I could tell by the sound of his heavy feet. "It's time."

The funeral was today. We would have the service at the church then transport his body to the cemetery nearby, placing him on top of my mother so they could be together for eternity. I'd watched him stop breathing, and that felt like the most final goodbye I could give. Going to the funeral would just destroy me even more—but I couldn't skip it.

Maverick was patient with me. He hadn't snapped at me since my father had passed away. He didn't go out of his way to be nice to me, but he didn't pick any fights either. He came farther into the room and approached the couch. "Arwen."

I didn't look up at him, the tears still coming.

He stood beside me, still like a statue.

I covered my eyes with my hand and took a deep breath, willing my tears to stop so I could make it to the church with a dry face. My fingers smeared away the final tears, and I rose to my feet. I avoided his gaze, embarrassed by the way my face must look right now, red and blotchy.

His arm circled my waist, and he guided me to the door. It was good that he was there because I still didn't know my way around this maze. He got me to the car and we drove away, heading to the church in the heart of the city.

Dante wouldn't be there because I couldn't make a public appearance with another man, especially when my father's enemies were ready to collect what they'd lost. My apartment was gone, and my bank accounts were closed. I didn't have a penny to my name—my maiden name.

Maverick looked out the window as we made the drive to the city.

I rested my head against the window and tried to stay positive. My father wouldn't want me to feel like this, to be this devastated. He would want me to accept his departure and know he'd lived a happy life.

But that was easier said than done.

EVERYONE WHO KNEW my father was in the church. They gave me their condolences and congratulated me on my wedding. Other people shed their tears for my father, so I wasn't the only one. Like any real husband would do, Maverick had his arm around my waist, being a public crutch to my misery.

We sat in the pews and listened to the service performed by the priest. I sat in the very front with Maverick by my side. We were the only people in the front because I was the only family he had left.

My fingers clutched the speech I'd written the night before. As his daughter, I should say something, tell everyone in that church what a great father he was. But the ink was splotched with my tears, and my hands shook because I couldn't keep my composure. I wasn't afraid to address hundreds of people inside a church.

I just didn't think I could stop crying long enough to get a few words out.

The priest then addressed me. "Now Martin's daughter, Arwen, has a few words to share with us."

I hadn't stopped crying, and the idea of saying the words I'd penned the night before broke my heart. He'd told me he had cancer less than two weeks ago. I had to accept his death in a short amount of time, but I hadn't accepted his departure enough to speak even somewhat coherently. I clutched the paper with a shaking hand and willed myself to rise to my feet and complete my duty.

But I couldn't move.

I couldn't stop crying.

All eyes were on me, and I was too depressed to even feel embarrassed.

Maverick took the paper from my hand and stood.

I stopped crying long enough to look up and see him walk up the steps to the pulpit, my speech in hand. In a black suit with a matching tie, he looked as handsome as he did on our wedding day. With dark eyes that matched his attire, he looked fit enough to be the model for his own line of cologne. Commanding the room in a way even the priest couldn't do, he stood at the pulpit and addressed everyone. "I'm Maverick DeVille, Arwen's husband." With broad shoulders and a calm façade, he looked out at all the people watching him, not the least bit intimidated by their stares. "My wife has been crippled by the loss, so I'll speak on her behalf. Before I read what she's written, I have a few words of my own. When I met Martin Chatel, the one thing that was most obvious to me was the love he had for his daughter. Nothing else mattered to him, and when he understood his days were limited, all he could think about was the wellbeing of his beloved Arwen. We'd intended to marry a year from now, but Martin said it would mean the world to him if he could walk his daughter down the aisle. He told me he would live long enough to see it through—but not much after. He was always kind to me, telling me how much he appreciated the way I cared for his daughter. His fatherly love was obvious to anyone who could feel, and I could feel it anytime I was in the room with him. Above all else, that is the greatest compliment I can give him. He was a good man—and an amazing father."

Tears continued to stream down my face, and I was so grateful that Maverick took the reins when I could barely stand. He was a much better speaker than I was—at least right now. If I were to speak, my words would be muffled by the sobs of sorrow that screamed out of my chest.

He surveyed everyone in the room then turned to the

note I'd written. He glanced it over and then he started to read from it. "Ever since I was a little girl, my father called me princess. He got me a plastic tiara, and I wore it every single day for an entire year. When I started school, I was told I had to leave it at home—because a princess doesn't always need her crown. Even when I became a grown woman, he never called me by any other name. I was always 'princess.' I don't know how I'll live the rest of my life without hearing that nickname again, but I know I'll always be his princess." Maverick tilted his head down and read the next paragraph, grasping what I wanted to say before he spoke again. "Watching him lose my mother was the hardest thing I've ever had to do. Once she was gone, he was never the same. He still loved me, but that light in his eyes was permanently gone the moment her soul left this earth. I try to remember that he's with her now, that they're finally together again—looking down on me. He wouldn't want me or anyone else to be so devastated by this loss. Even at a time when he was barely able to get out of bed, he put a smile on his face, put on his suit, and walked me down the aisle like it was the happiest day of his life—not mine. I'll miss my father for so many reasons, but the biggest reason of all—he was my closest friend. But one day I'll see him again. It may be a long time from now, but once my soul leaves this earth, I'll find his and mother's once again—and we'll be a family. On that day, he'll smile and once again call me his princess." Maverick folded the note and slipped it into his pocket before he left the pulpit and returned to his seat. As if he hadn't just helped me in my time of need, he stared straight ahead like nothing unusual had happened.

I didn't understand this man at all. Sometimes he was

cruel. Sometimes he was kind. He was an enigma, an absolute mystery. I would have to appreciate his good moments and push through the bad. My hand reached for his on his thigh, and I interlocked our fingers. "Thank you."

He didn't say a word. Instead, he squeezed my hand in acknowledgment.

EVERYONE HAD LEFT THE GRAVESITE. I was the only one who lingered, unable to leave both my parents buried in the soil for all eternity. I was their only remnant of mortality, their only connection to this world.

I stayed there for so long that the sun started to set on the horizon, taking the heat with it. Everyone else had left in their cars a long time ago, unable to bear the summer temperatures.

Maverick stayed near the road, giving me the space to mourn my father in private. The driver waited for us to finish our afternoon, and while Maverick could have left without me and sent someone back to pick me up, he waited.

Maybe he wasn't as much of an asshole as I'd thought.

Minutes later, he walked across the grass and came to my side. We were alone together now, so there was no need to put on a show, to pretend we were newlyweds suffering through a tragedy together.

But he moved his arm around my waist anyway. "It's getting late. We can stay a few more minutes, but we should get going." He was the gentlest he'd ever been, not ordering me around like he had in the past.

"It hurts to leave him here. When I walk away...it'll really be final. This day will come to a close, my father will be dead, and then I'll move on…" I unclenched the tissue in my hand and wiped my nose.

"He'd want you to move on."

"I know…it's just hard."

His hand started to move up my back, gently massaging my muscles through the thin material of my dress.

"Don't forget where he really is. Physically, he may be in the ground. But his soul is up there…with your mother. He's moved on—and so should you."

I wiped my tears away with my tissue then clutched it in my hand once more. "Is that where you think your mother is?"

His hand paused in the middle of my back. "If there is a heaven, that's exactly where she is."

13

MAVERICK

Life went on for everyone else, but for Arwen, her whole world seemed to stop.

She stayed in her room day after day, preferring solitude and the memories that haunted her. Sometimes she took the meals that Abigail sent, but she rejected all the rest. Everyone handled grief differently, but she handled it like someone had poured acid over her eyes.

I shouldn't care about her condition. When she was locked in her room, she left me alone. It was like she didn't exist at all. I returned to working, drinking, and fucking like I didn't have a wife on the second floor.

But she kept popping up in my mind.

I guess I missed the fiery woman who screamed at me outside the opera house. I missed the woman who told off my father without batting an eyelash. I missed the woman in the painting.

I walked to the second floor and approached her bedroom. It'd been four days since I'd last seen her, and Abigail reported to me that she'd spent her time sleeping, taking baths, and watching TV. She hadn't left her bedroom once.

I rapped my knuckles against the door.

Her response was solemn. "I'm not hungry, Abigail."

I let myself inside and found her standing in front of her closet, wearing a purple dress as she slipped on her sandals. Her purse was on her shoulder like she intended to leave the house even though it was almost eight. "Going somewhere?"

She righted herself and turned to look at me. "I'm sleeping at Dante's tonight."

Dante was the guy I'd seen at the hospital. He was a good-looking guy, tall, but not muscular the way I was. He was also the same guy in her bed, the one who wanted to marry her until I came into the picture.

She came toward me, her hair and makeup done. Her spirit had improved, but there was still distinct melancholy in her gaze. But she must be in a better mood if she was ready to leave the house for the first time. "I'll be home in the morning. I took some time off from the opera, but they're expecting me again tomorrow night."

I couldn't ask her to stay because that's not what we agreed on, but I felt odd letting her leave my property on her own and venturing into the city to be with her lover. But I was just with someone last night, fucking until my headboard made another dent in the wall. I had to let her go because it wouldn't be right to ask her to stay. "Alright. I'll give you a long overdue tour of the house tomorrow. And if you're interested, you can see the factory where we produce, mix, and age the cheese." It was a family business that had been handed down for generations. Now it was in my hands because my father had other ambitions that had nothing to do with food.

"Yeah...that sounds nice."

I continued to stand in the doorway, but I had no idea what kept me there.

She glanced at the door then looked at me again. "Something wrong?"

"Abigail told me you haven't left your room in four days. I wasn't sure if I should be concerned or not."

"It's been hard...but I'm a little better now. I don't think I can cry anymore."

The funeral and the days that followed were her darkest. A part of me actually pitied her, seeing the way she crumbled into so many pieces. I didn't have the nerve to be a dick because it seemed so harsh at the time. Her tears actually made me feel terrible... Maybe that was why I hated it when she cried.

"Thank you for everything you did at the funeral." She dropped her gaze as she held on to her purse, like she was remembering all the events in the privacy behind her eyes. "That was so hard for me, and you were...my rock."

Publicly, I was her husband and I acted that way. But I also saw an innocent woman going through a difficult time. Her father screwed her over then died right afterward, taking the easy way out. Now she had to live with the consequences of his stupidity...it wasn't fair.

"And what you said about my father at the funeral...that was really nice."

I didn't come here expecting her gratitude. I let the words bounce off me.

She waited for me to acknowledge what she said, but

when nothing happened, she dropped it. "I'll see you tomorrow, then." She maneuvered past me and walked out the bedroom door.

I didn't turn around to watch her leave. I focused on the sound of her footsteps, listening to them trail away until she was gone.

I WAS asleep when my phone rang on the nightstand.

No one would be stupid enough to call me at this time of night, so whatever it was, it was important.

Becky moaned at the sound, kicking me under the sheets.

I answered the call without checking who it was. "Maverick."

"Sir, it's Liam down at the gate." Liam was the head of my security for the property. My estate didn't just include my private property where my residence was. It also included the factory where we produced the high-quality cheese that was distributed all across Europe. I had a large territory to maintain and protect.

"What is it?" My eyes were still closed because I was half asleep.

Becky moaned like she wanted me to be quiet.

"A group of men pulled up in a Hummer. Five armed guys. The leader is asking for you. His name is Kamikaze."

Not that asshole.

"The gate is locked and they haven't tried to enter the premises, but he's asking for you. Says you can face him now, or you can face him later—your choice."

Kamikaze was basically the devil. He made underground

deals all over the world, commissioning the sale of weapons, humans, drugs, and anything else you could think of. He was a third party in commerce—but not the middle man you could just cut out. I'd done business with him before—only a handful of times. "Did he say what he wanted?"

"No."

I didn't want to send him away so he could sneak up on me later. I would just lie there in bed and wonder what was going on in my own front yard. I didn't appreciate his unexpected visit, but when someone raised the stakes, I had to do the same. "I'll be there in five minutes."

I WALKED down the driveway and approached the closed gates. My hair had been hastily styled with my fingertips and I'd washed the sleep out of my eyes, so I looked like I'd been up at three a.m. like these assholes. "Open the gate." I had armed men all over the place, and these guys obviously didn't want a war if they only had five men altogether. Just because they were armed didn't mean they were hostile—all men were armed.

The iron gates swung inward and opened onto the dirt path that extended a quarter mile before it connected to the main road.

Kamikaze was in the front, with his big, square head and nearly seven feet in height. His arms bulged with pounds of muscle, and he looked suited for war. A shotgun was draped across his back, like he was prepared to blow someone to pieces in close proximity.

His size didn't scare me. "This better be important to

show up on my doorstep like this. Drop your phone in the toilet?"

Kamikaze smiled, showing all of his white teeth. Combined with his large cow-like eyes, his grin looked maniacal. He stepped closer to me, ignoring all the guns trained directly on his forehead. "It's very important. Martin Chatel cost me millions—and now he's dead."

In the back of my mind, this is what I'd feared. The hounds were on the scent and looking for someone to blame for their loses. This was the price I had to pay to avenge my mother. I had to protect Arwen from this double-decker bus. "Explain how that concerns me."

He stepped closer. "Because you married his little bitch."

I kept my gaze locked on him, my chin angled up because he was five inches taller than me. I was considered to be a big man, six three with two hundred pounds of muscle. But this guy was a fucking mutant. What the hell was Martin thinking, making a deal with this freak? "I don't see the relevance."

"Don't be coy with me. That bastard set me back millions—hundreds of millions. The banks took all of his possessions, and I'm the one left hanging."

"Then you should have gotten some collateral."

He came even closer to me. "She *is* the collateral."

I didn't move an inch, not backing down to any man. He may be bigger, but I still had the upper hand.

"The sins of the father are not the sins of the daughter. She had no idea what he was doing with their money. He lost everything—and so did she. You want to take her for all she's got, but she's broke."

"She's not broke anymore...not when she's married to you."

"I'm not giving you anything, Kamikaze. You already knew that before you came here, so I hope you have something better to say."

He cocked his head slightly. "I do, actually. I want her."

"Her? As in my wife?"

"Yes. You already knew that, so I hope you have something better to say." He echoed my own words back at me, knowing I was trying to downplay this as much as possible.

"I'm not giving her to you. And even if I did, it doesn't fix your problem."

"That's where you're wrong. A beautiful woman like that could be sold for tens of millions, if not more. She could work off her debt to me—one fuck at a time. With tits like that and pipes that can shatter glass, men would pay a lot for her. And I'm not the only man Martin screwed over—so men would pay a fortune for their revenge."

Arwen would fight him hard, and that resilience would only make her more desirable. I hadn't fucked her, but I could understand the desire. She was beautiful, curvy, and she could definitely sing. "I'm not giving you my wife. Come near her, and I'll kill you."

"I understand you had nothing to do with Martin's idiocy. I'm an honorable guy. You think I'd just take her from you?"

We had different definitions of honorable.

"No," he said with a laugh. "I'll pay you for her. That's fair."

If she knew this conversation was taking place, she would lose her shit.

"I'll give you a very generous offer—five million."

Martin was dead, and I had the information I needed to kill Ramon. It would be easy to hand her off and go back to my old life—along with some change in my pocket. But I'd made a promise to that man—and I would keep it. "No."

His eyes narrowed in displeasure. "Ten."

"Let me save you some time. She's not for sale." I turned back to the gate, dismissing the conversation. "I'm sorry the deal with Martin went south. But my wife isn't for sale—for any price."

I SAT at the dining table staring out the window that over-looked the backyard, the space where we held the wedding. I could have rented out the most beautiful church in the city or picked another place to hold the ceremony, but the grounds of my estate were perfect. And since we had the wedding on such short notice, it was our only option.

I sipped my coffee and opened the newspaper.

Footsteps sounded behind me, a pace that was far too quick for Abigail. She always moved around the house at a remarkable speed, but she somehow seemed so poised and calm as she did. Her shoes wouldn't make such a ruckus. So it could only be one person.

In the same clothes she'd worn the night before, Arwen entered the dining room. "Morning." She placed her purse on the table and took a seat, her makeup gone and her hair a little messier than it was when she left last night.

It was the first time I'd seen her not wearing pounds of mascara and thick eyeliner. With the foundation gone, her complexion really shone through, unblemished and beauti-ful. Her skin was lovely, and her eyes seemed to stand out even more when she was bare.

She poured herself a cup of coffee then added two cubes of sugar.

I stared at her for another moment before I turned back to my newspaper. I didn't ask about her night because I didn't give a damn. While she was getting fucked by Dante, I was fucking what's-her-name.

She stirred her coffee and took a drink. "How was your night?"

A group of assholes showed up at my doorstep and caused trouble. So, it was pretty shitty. "Fine." I still didn't ask about hers.

She seemed to understand I was in a mood, so she stopped asking questions.

Good. She was learning.

My date for the evening walked into the room when she finally woke up. "Sorry I slept in so late. After you left in the middle of the night, I couldn't get back to sleep." With her shoes in her hand and messy hair, she didn't even give Arwen a second glance. She knew I was married, but since I'd told her we had an open relationship, she didn't bother being discreet. She leaned over me and kissed me on the neck. "Call me later."

Once a woman asked me to call her, I never did. When expectations were established, I lost interest.

She walked out and left us to enjoy our breakfast.

Abigail brought in the plates then went back to the kitchen.

Arwen didn't ask about the woman I'd spent the night with. "Did you leave last night?"

I didn't lie to make my life easier. It was too much work because you had to keep track of every lie you ever told. I'd rather just be honest and piss people off. But if I told Arwen about Kamikaze, it would terrify her. The woman had already been through enough in the last two weeks. I wasn't going to tell her some assholes wanted to buy her and sell her into sexual slavery. "Pipe busted on the grounds. I had to fix it."

"Don't you have men for that?"

I looked up from my newspaper. "I'm quicker."

She set down her coffee and started to eat. She must be in a better mood because she hadn't had an appetite recently. A long night with Dante seemed to recharge her.

I didn't know anything about Dante, but he didn't seem good enough for her. They weren't going to last, so I guess it didn't matter anyway. "You're at the theater tonight?"

"Yes. For practice."

I folded my newspaper then straightened so I could eat my breakfast while it was still hot.

She smeared Abigail's homemade jam across her toast and took a bite, rolling her eyes just a little bit like she couldn't believe how good it was. "I love jam..." After a few more bites, she ate the entire thing then moved on to her eggs.

I didn't expect us to eat together every morning, but she seemed to have invited herself to share the ritual with me. I'd tell her to leave, but it was too soon to be a jackass. When enough time passed, I could start to be myself again.

"Are you still going to give me a tour of the house? I can barely remember how to get to my room."

"If you're up for it."

"Definitely. I've never told you this before, but your home is beautiful."

Her family estate used to be glorious at one time, but now

it was long gone. The banks would remove anything they could sell, and it would be put on the market for someone else to purchase. Her ancestral home had been passed down for generations—and now it would belong to someone else.

She sipped her coffee. "You really can't take a compliment, can you?"

I took a bite of my food and stared her down, chewing slowly as I considered what to say. Threatening her was my automatic response, but I was still trying to be sensitive because of her father's passing.

She smeared more jam onto her toast. "When you don't like something, you just ignore it?"

"Would you rather have me yell at you?"

"No. I just wish I understood why you refuse to acknowledge every positive thing I say."

"If you're fishing for a response to every compliment you give, then it must not be genuine."

"It is genuine. I'm just trying to understand you."

I brought my coffee to my lips and took a drink. "Save yourself some time and don't."

I TOOK her on a tour of the house, showing her the large kitchen Abigail thrived in, the three separate dining rooms, the different living rooms, and then the private gym on the second floor.

She looked at the cardio machines and all the equipment I used on a daily basis. "Wow. This is the size of a regular gym. You're the only one who uses it?"

"You can use it too if you like."

"I'm not big on exercise." She walked to the biceps curl and stared at the machine like she had no idea how it worked. "Singing is my exercise."

Then she must have good genes, keeping a figure like that. I'd only seen her eat a couple of times, and she had a full meal. I walked out of the gym then took her to the drawing room on the third floor. The room didn't have much of a purpose, but it had the best view of the property. There were a couple of couches facing each other and a grand piano tucked into the corner. Sleek and black, it didn't have a spot of dust because my staff kept this entire place perfectly tidy every single day.

Her eyes lit up when she spotted the instrument. "Maverick, do you play?" She approached the piano and slid her hand along the smooth exterior, touching the glossy finish. She moved to the bench and lightly pressed her fingers against the keys, exploring the whites and the blacks.

"No."

"Then why do you have it?" She tested out the notes, as if she were checking that the piano was still in tune.

"Ask my interior decorator."

I had a lot of priceless possessions in this house, but this seemed to be the only thing that truly impressed her. With a loving gaze, she stared at the keys and made love to each one with her fingertips. Gentle sounds filled the room, random notes that didn't create a song.

I watched her head dip to observe the movement of her fingers, watched the way she instantly became immersed in the instrument, like she was about to perform on stage. Her eyes filled with innate joy, like this was the first time she'd felt happiness since her father passed away.

"Do you play?" It felt like a stupid question when I saw how attached she'd already become.

"Yes." She hesitantly pulled her hands away from the keyboard and rose to her feet. "Can I play it sometime? When I'm rehearsing?"

The question seemed odd considering this was her home now, but my bedroom was right down the hallway so I could probably hear every sound she made. "This is your home now. Do whatever you want."

———

WE DROVE a golf cart to the factory a few acres away. The facility had workers that showed up every day, stirring the cheese in the big pots, melting the wax onto the cheese wheel, and professionals dating and storing the cheese until they were properly aged. They had to check in with security at the gate every day before they came onto the property.

Arwen was fascinated by everything.

I took her through the factory, showing her the different parts of the assembly. "Our cheese is native to Italy because we have special bacteria that is indigenous to the area. It doesn't grow anywhere else in the known world." I stood off to the side with her as two men stirred the cheese wheel that was forming in the center of the pot. "We inoculate our cows with it, and that produces the special milk we use to make the cheese." We kept moving through the factory, seeing the different steps until we arrived at the storage room. Hundreds of cheese wheels were stacked high in their cubbies.

Arwen walked down the aisle and examined one at eye level. "This is humongous. Do people buy the entire wheel?"

"Yes. Mainly restaurants."

"That must be expensive. It's got to weigh twenty pounds."

"It is expensive. They can range from two to four thousand euros."

Even though she'd been rich all her life, her eyes still filled with surprise. "Wow...how long are they aged?"

"The minimum is three years. But we have cheese wheels that are ten years old. The longer they age, the more they're worth." I kept walking and headed to the very rear of the building, stepping inside the large office where I took care of the business.

She followed behind me, examining my oversize desk and the bookshelves on both walls. She picked up a book at random and glanced at the title, seeing that it was a manufacturing book about the cheese process. She turned it then looked at my mahogany desk. Behind it was a picture window with my three-story home in the distance. "How long has the business been in your family?"

"Longer than I can remember. At least ten generations."

"Wow...even some of the historic wineries don't date back that far. That's amazing." She studied my plain desk, seeing the closed laptop that sat in the center. There was nothing else on the surface besides a single pen. "You're extremely organized."

"Minimalist."

When she looked out the window and admired the house in the distance, the sunlight blanketed her face perfectly, making those blue eyes shine like they were two orbs. With her arms across her chest, she stood there for nearly a minute before she turned away. "If you ever need any help, I'm happy to lend you a hand. I don't know much, but I'm a fast learner and a hard worker."

My business was self-sufficient. It worked on a tight schedule, and I oversaw the big things. My foreman was in charge of all the day-to-day stuff. I never expected her to be part of my world. "I have all the help I need."

"Alright...the offer still stands if you ever change your mind."

———————

WHEN WE RETURNED to the house, she turned to me. "You didn't show me your office."

"I just did."

"Your home office."

"I don't see why you need to see that." Or my bedroom.

Her nostrils flared like she was irritated by the comment, but she held back her rebuttal, being more compatible because I'd been nice to her. She swallowed her retorts and kept the peace instead of insulting me like I deserved. It was a diplomatic move for her. "I'm going to take a nap before I head out for the show." She headed to the stairs. "I'll see you later." When she got to the point where she couldn't stand me anymore, she made a good excuse to get away from me.

I watched her ass move back and forth as she climbed the stairs with a straight back. It was strange to think that I would have to share my life with this woman, that I should probably show her my office. In my mind, I kept thinking this was short-term, but it wasn't.

It was a lifelong commitment.

I caught up with her. "Follow me."

On the second landing, she turned to me, clearly uneasy about what I wanted.

"Come on." I took the lead and moved to the third floor. I didn't check if she was behind me because the sound of her shoes was audible enough. I went past the bright windows and approached the door across the hall from my bedroom. "This is my office." I stepped inside the large room. There were two couches that faced the dark desk situated near the window. Decorated in dark colors with a stash of brandy and scotch in plain sight, it was my personal space. There was a box of cigars on the table.

She stepped inside, and the first thing she noticed was the cigars. "You smoke?"

"Occasionally."

She didn't take a seat as she examined my room, her arms crossed over her chest like she was afraid to let her guard down in my presence. "It suits you…"

I grabbed the decanter of brandy and two glasses. "Would you like some?"

"I'm not a brandy kind of girl."

"Water, then?"

"No, I'll take the scotch." I paused for just an instant as I set the glasses on my desk. She seemed like a girl who could only handle a weak bottle of wine. I would have never guessed that she had a palate for something stronger. I swapped out the brandy for the scotch and filled both glasses.

She took a seat then accepted the drink. Bringing it to her lips, she took a decent swallow and didn't even cringe when the booze dropped into her stomach. With perfect posture and crossed legs, she sat like she was still every bit of royalty.

I sat across from her and grabbed a cigar. "Mind if I smoke?"

"As long as you don't smoke alone."

I stilled again, not expecting her to participate in such a disgusting habit. She seemed like a woman who would berate me for smoking, because she was a perfect know-it-all. Or maybe she just didn't care how long I lived.

She placed the cigar in her mouth, her full lips snug around the tip. She leaned forward and craned her neck out, the front of her dress giving way and revealing cleavage that was impossible to ignore.

But I didn't look. I held the lighter to the end until it started to burn. She sucked at the same time, making the ash smolder into orange embers. With two fingers, she pulled the cigar out of her mouth and let a wall of smoke rise to the ceiling.

I was so mesmerized, I almost forgot to light my own cigar. I'd never seen a woman smoke like that, at least not a woman of her station. She seemed too prissy for it. I got the end burning and brought the smoke into my mouth, immediately feeling the calming sensation as it absorbed into my blood. I released a deep breath and let the smoke escape my nostrils.

With her drink in one hand and the cigar in the other, she leaned back against the couch and got comfortable, looking just like one of the guys. She slowly puffed on her cigar and let the smoke rise to the high, vaulted ceiling.

I hated to admit it, but she looked pretty sexy.

I left my drink on the table and moved to my desk to retrieve the folder. I returned and set the cigar in the ashtray so I could go over the papers. "This is for you." I pulled out a couple bank cards and set them in front of her. "This one is for monthly expenses, gas, food, shopping, whatever." I pushed another toward her. "This is for emergencies, and if you need to make a purchase up to a million dollars. If you need more cash than that, you'll have to get approval from me —and I'll probably say no." I picked up the cigar again and took another puff.

She eyed the cards without taking them. "I don't need this."

She was broke, so unless Dante was buying her everything, she didn't have any cash. "I think you do."

"I get paid from the opera. It's not a fortune, but it's enough to cover food, gas, and anything else I might need. I don't have rent or a car payment, and all my meals at the house are free. It's a nice gesture, but I don't need your money." She set her cigar in the ashtray and changed her focus to the scotch.

I just threw a ton of money at her, and she turned it down. No one in their right mind would do that. "You should still keep these in case you need them." If she really did pay for her own things, then it wouldn't be like she existed at all. She was just a woman who slept in one of the rooms and shared meals with me. She could have easily taken the cards and gone on a shopping spree, but she didn't seem interested. She was used to being rich, but now she didn't seem to care that she wasn't anymore.

She left them on the table but didn't argue with me.

"How much do you make at the opera?"

She took a long drink then licked her lips. "Maybe a thousand euro every two weeks."

"That's nothing."

"I don't have any bills, so it's plenty. Otherwise, I would just put the money into your account anyway."

I wouldn't take a dime from her.

"So, I'll just cash my checks and spend that."

I'd dreaded marrying this woman, but now it didn't seem so bad. She didn't rip into my wallet right away, and she did make an effort to be nice to me...even if it annoyed me sometimes. She could never get me to like her, but she was getting me to respect her—which was impressive. "Your name is on one of my accounts, so you can go to the bank if you need something."

"Why would you do that?" she asked, dead serious. "Maverick, I don't need your wealth. I'm only here because I need the protection. But I don't need your money, and I certainly don't need to be on your account." She sipped her drink again then eyed her cigar.

I closed the folder and picked up my cigar again. "How long have you smoked?"

She took a deep puff and let the smoke rise from her mouth and drift toward the ceiling. "A few years. I only do it once in a while...maybe two times a year."

So, much rarer than I did.

"You?"

"I've been smoking for ten years."

"And how often?"

"Weekly."

She didn't give me a judgmental stare, but there was a slight pursing of her lips. "That's not good. You should cut back."

"I should do whatever I want." There were so many things in this world that could kill me. I chose to live how I wanted, and that was on the dangerous side. I finished the scotch and left the glass on the empty table before I rested against the cushion of the couch.

"How old are you?"

The question was unexpected, and it also indicated how little she knew about me. Given how angry she was at her father at the time, she'd probably never had the opportunity to ask about me—especially since she'd refused to marry me. "Almost thirty."

"That could mean anything. That could be twenty-six."

"Twenty-nine." And my birthday was on Saturday. When I said almost, I meant it literally. I didn't know anything about her either, other than the fact that she was an opera singer, and that was only because her father took me to a performance. I'd never cared to learn about her either because she would never mean anything to me. "How old are you?"

"Twenty-two."

Jesus, she was young. This woman was almost ten years younger than me. I never would have guessed it, not because her appearance suggested she was close to my age, but because she possessed the attitude of someone much older. She had wisdom, she had grace, she wasn't an obnoxious party girl that had only been drinking for a couple years.

"So, you're an old man." A slight smile stretched across her lips, like she was teasing me.

With the amount of shit I'd seen, I certainly felt like an old man. "I feel like one."

Her firm legs were crossed at the knee, her slender calves noticeable underneath her dress. Her skin reminded me of the color of my cheese, just before it was covered in the wax seal and stored on the wooden shelves. It was such a beautiful color, like a blush rose petal that had never been harmed by the sun's damaging rays. I forced my eyes down into my drink, careful not to stare at her.

"My father never explained your role in the underworld. It seems like you and your father have bloody hands."

"We aren't different from everyone else. Sometimes we make illegal trades, sometimes we buy things that shouldn't be for sale, sometimes we break the rules just for the hell of it. My father and I used to be more involved in drug trafficking across the shore to Turkey. There's a lot of money in that. But things started to get too serious, and we were in too deep. We built a reputation for ourselves because we never let anything stand in our way. But all of that changed when we pissed off Ramon and he wanted revenge. So he crossed the line and took my mother. We got out of the game and never went back." It had been a stupid decision on our part all along because we didn't need the money in the first place. Our greed cost us my mother's life. All that money we'd made was covered in her blood now. It was tainted.

"I'm sorry." Even when she wasn't singing, she had the most beautiful voice. It was whimsical, somehow musical. She could express her emotions so easily because the sound of her voice was so heavy with her thoughts. So when she whispered those words, it was obvious she meant them. "When will you kill him?"

"Next week. Your father had contact with one of his suppliers. That's how he knew he would be returning to Florence. My father and I have been trying to track him down for a year, but since he was hiding in Croatia, it was too difficult. But now we have our chance."

"I hope you get what you want—and it gives you closure."

Killing Ramon wouldn't bring my mother back, but it had to be done anyway.

"Have you talked to your father lately?"

"I avoid him like the plague."

"I don't blame you." She finished her scotch then set the glass on the table. Her cigar was still burning, so she took another puff then left it in the ashtray. A string of smoke escaped from her lips.

When I'd stepped into that hospital room and watched Dante leave, I didn't like him immediately. A real man wouldn't have allowed her to marry someone else. He wouldn't have given up on her. A woman like this should have been with a man who could have protected her from Kamikaze and all the other assholes that hated her father. That was how I knew Dante wasn't good enough for her—not even close. "What do you see in him?"

It took her a moment to understand the question. Her eyebrows rose slowly as she regarded me, deducing exactly who I was talking about. "What's that supposed to mean?"

"Doesn't seem like your type."

"And you know my type?" she questioned.

"I just assumed you were interested in men—not boys."

Sparks flew in her eyes. "Dante is a good man, and I might have married him if this hadn't happened. He's kind and good to me. He's much better than that trashy woman who didn't bother putting on her shoes before walking out the door."

I didn't take offense to that because I didn't give a damn about what's-her-name. "She means nothing to me, so I don't care if she is trashy. But you love this guy, so it's a different story. If he really loved you, he wouldn't have stepped aside and let you marry someone else. That's why I don't understand what you see in him."

"I never said I loved him."

"You said you would have married him."

"I said I *might* have married him if things were different. We only met a few months ago, so we didn't have much time together before all of this happened. And I never would have wanted him to interfere because it would have cost him his life."

"And if he were your man, he wouldn't have cared."

Her eyes narrowed. "You don't seem like the kind of man that's ever been in love, so you shouldn't talk about it like you understand it."

"I'm not talking about love. I'm talking about being a man —two very different things. And in my eyes, Dante is no man." I rose to my feet and left the glasses and ashtray on the table. "Fuck whoever you want—but I think you can do better." I moved around her couch and headed to the door.

"That's ironic," she said without turning around. "I could say the same about you."

14

ARWEN

For the next few days, I worked at the opera and slept at Dante's. Annoyed by Maverick's comments, I avoided him. His opinion shouldn't matter to me, but I was tired of trying to lay a tolerable foundation between us and have him destroy it every time. Just when I thought I could talk to him, he proved me wrong.

It was hard to believe he was the man who'd held my hand through my father's funeral, the man who'd acted as my crutch to survive those horrible days. Unexpectedly, he could be the most compassionate man I'd ever met—but he could turn on you.

I went to the theater that night and performed, getting lost in the music as I played to an audience I couldn't see. The stage lights were so bright on my face that everything in the background was just darkness.

But it still made me feel alive.

Singing had been my passion since I could remember. Now I used it to nurse my broken heart, to focus on something so my mind wouldn't drift away. Everything in my life had changed drastically—this was the only thing that stayed the same.

When the curtains closed, Dante came backstage, roses in his hand.

I smiled at the gesture and resisted the urge to kiss him since I had to be discreet with my affairs now. But I knew my emotions were written on my face; I was grateful that this man was still around. He was the only remaining person from my former life, a reminder of how my life used to be.

"You were amazing. I could watch you sing forever."

"Thank you."

"Want to have dinner at my place?"

"There's no place I'd rather go."

WE ATE at his dining table, enjoying the food that was delivered to the apartment. We couldn't go out anymore because we couldn't be seen together. Our time together was spent in this apartment, mainly in his bed. It started to feel like an affair as time passed. It started off as a relationship—but now it was just a secret.

He stopped eating and set his fork down, his eyes filled with troubling thoughts. He didn't wear that handsome smile or show affection in his eyes. Something weighed his shoulders down, haunted him.

I knew what it was. And I knew what was coming.

"I can't do this anymore…" He lifted his gaze and looked at me, apology in his eyes. "You used to be mine, and now I have to share you. Every time we're in bed together, I have to see the ring on your finger. Every time we're in public, I have to pretend to be just your friend..."

Even though I knew this was coming, it still hurt.

"I know you aren't sleeping with him and I trust you, but I still feel like the other man."

I wanted to fight for us, to tell him nothing had changed. But I cared too much about him to persuade him to stay with me. All of his points were valid. He wanted the real thing, a real relationship. I couldn't give him that.

"We can never go out to dinner, hang out with my friends...do anything. And I met this woman..."

Now it really started to hurt.

"I told her I was seeing someone, so nothing has happened. But being around her makes me realize what I want... I'm sorry."

He wanted her—not me.

"I wish things could be different."

I wasn't going to cry over a man. I'd cried so much in the last few weeks that my tear ducts were spent. He wasn't worth my heartache. If he wanted to be with someone else, then it was over before I even saw him this evening. Maybe Maverick was right. Maybe this man wasn't good enough for me. If he really loved me, he would love me despite the restrictions...or he would fight for me. Dante wanted to do neither. "I understand, Dante. You're completely right. This isn't a relationship, it's an affair." It was just sex behind closed doors. All the romance died when I forced Dante to be a secret. I swallowed my pain and my pride and just let it be.

He rested his hand on mine. "I really am sorry. I know you've been through so much—"

"Really, I'm fine. Please don't feel bad for me." I looked

him in the eye to give my words more credibility. "This is my life, not yours. There's no reason for you to drown just because I'm obligated to go down with the ship."

Dante studied me, true pain in his eyes. He clearly hated this conversation, hated to hurt me.

Despite what he'd just done, I knew he was a good guy. He would make a woman very happy. He would be a faithful husband and a good father. With enough time, he would forget about me entirely and struggle to remember when there was someone else in his life besides his wife. That was how it should be.

And he deserved that.

I CLEARED security at the gate at one in the morning.

I drove to the house up the road and pulled into the enormous garage that housed his expensive toys. Instead of driving a Bugatti or a Ferrari, I drove a Mercedes. He offered something more luxurious, but I didn't want a car I was terrified to drive.

I slipped off my heels and walked into the house, relieved it was so quiet. Abigail had gone to bed, and the rest of the servants went home for the day. That allowed me to take my time going up the stairs, to let my shoulders sag from the sadness and exhaustion.

I made it to the second landing and almost bumped right into Maverick.

In just his sweatpants, barefoot and bare-chested, he stood in my way, his tanned skin tight over strong muscles. The veins ran all the way from the tops of his arms to his hands, a design of webs that showed just how fit his physique really was. His skin had its own smolder, like a drop of water would immediately turn to steam because he naturally ran so hot. His hair was a little messy because he'd obviously been sleeping when I pulled up to the house. The slightly tired look in his eyes was somehow sexy, probably because he had to let his guard down to fall asleep. "Why are you home so late?"

I didn't feel like being interrogated right now. I walked around him and headed to my room, my heels in one hand and my purse in the other. "You said I could come and go as I wished."

His footsteps sounded as he followed me. "You told me you wouldn't be home until tomorrow."

"Well, I changed my mind. What's the big deal?" I made it to my bedroom and stepped through the doorway.

He joined me, coming inside, something he rarely did. "It's a big deal because my security calls me every time someone drives to the gate past ten."

I opened my closet and slid the heels inside their cubby. "Then tell them not to call you."

He walked right up to me, clearly growing furious by my dismissal of everything he said. "Don't be smart with me. Don't tell me you aren't coming home and then pull up at one in the morning."

"I'm sorry," I said sarcastically. "I didn't realize my own home was off-limits to me."

"Just don't say one thing and do another."

"Well, shit happens." I tossed my purse on a shelf and stepped away from him.

He watched me walk away, his muscular arms resting by

his sides. His unnaturally tight stomach looked harder than a slab of concrete. A knife couldn't even penetrate his exterior because he was so hard. He made Dante seem soft, even though he was also a fit man. "What kind of shit would make you walk to your car by yourself and drive here in the middle of the night?"

I didn't want to give Maverick the satisfaction of being right, but the truth would come out eventually. Why not now? "Dante dumped me." I fell into the chair and crossed my legs, doing my best to ignore his focused stare. "He was tired of being a secret and found somebody else. I wasn't going to stay there a second longer. If I'd known I couldn't come here, I would have slept in my car." I knew Maverick would gloat about his assessment of Dante, calling him a boy. He would kick me while I was down, rise victorious in my ashes. It wasn't like me to avoid someone's gaze, but I couldn't bear to see the arrogance on his face.

Maverick stood still for a while before he moved to the spot beside me on the couch. Just like at the funeral when we were surrounded by watching eyes, he sat right beside me, his thigh touching mine. The second he was next to me, I could smell his lingering cologne, the cotton from his sheets. He didn't smell like a woman, so I assumed he'd been in bed alone tonight.

I continued to stare at the cold fireplace, hoping he would just leave and we would never discuss this night ever again.

His next words were surprising. "I'm sorry."

Just when I thought the worst of him, he surprised me.

"He was the last person from your former life…and losing him must be difficult."

I was shocked Maverick understood my feelings so well.

Losing a boyfriend wasn't the difficult part. It was losing all the pieces that used to comprise my old life. Now everything had fallen away, and I was a whole new person...a person I didn't like.

"But he wasn't good enough for you anyway, Arwen. At least you aren't wasting any more time."

"All I have is time to waste. There's nothing to look forward to. I'll never meet a man and fall in love. I'll never hit the milestones that other people do. I'm married and I'm rich —but I don't have anything." My life was empty.

"That's not true...you have me."

I finally turned my gaze and looked at him, surprised by what he'd said.

"I promised your father I would protect you—and that's what I'll do. You may feel alone in the world, but you do have that. We may not love each other or even like each other. But we're still allies."

And just like that, my opinion of him shifted. There was a big, beautiful heart inside that hard chest—he just hid it most of the time. His words could be so hurtful, but sometimes, they could be so beautiful. "Sometimes I don't know if I hate you or I like you...but right now, I like you."

He showed a slight smile, a rare sight. "Wait until tomorrow...you'll change your mind again."

FROM WHAT I GATHERED, Maverick woke up early every morning, worked out, had breakfast, and then went to work at the building on the other side of his property. He was hardly around the house during the day, and if he wasn't at work, I wasn't sure where he went.

We didn't see each other that much.

Sometimes I wondered if Maverick and I could be friends. Maybe we could do stuff together instead of sharing breakfast once in a while. But I remembered his kindness was used sparingly. If I hit a low point, he was there for me. He dropped his hostility and became the shoulder I needed to cry on. But once I was myself again, he turned back to the coldhearted jerk who didn't mince his words.

I spent a few days recovering from my breakup with Dante, trying not to imagine what his new love interest looked like. Was she a brunette too? Was she interesting? Had he already slept with her? I told myself it didn't matter, because deep down inside, I knew Dante made the right decision. He couldn't stay with me just to make me feel better. He needed to move on with his life—because he deserved a full life.

It was just depressing to know I would never have the same thing.

On Saturday, I was performing at the theatre, so I did my hair and makeup and prepared to leave, hoping I would run into Maverick before I left. I hadn't seen him in a few days. Since he was the only person who knew what I was going through, he was my confidant...not that he wanted to listen to my problems.

When I approached the stairs, I ran into Abigail. She had a small plate in her hands with a cupcake in the center. With chocolate frosting and a single candle, it looked like a miniature birthday cake.

"What's that for?" She brought food to my room during

my darkest days, but now that I'd been feeling better, I came to the dining table whenever meals were ready. It wouldn't make sense for her to bring a treat.

"Mr. DeVille. It's his birthday today. He hates to celebrate, but I always like to leave this on his nightstand…just to acknowledge it subtly. He never mentions it, but he does eat it…so I think he appreciates it."

"Today is his birthday?" I asked in surprise. He'd said he was turning thirty soon, but I'd had no idea how soon.

"Yes." She kept walking and headed to the next set of stairs.

"Is he home?"

"No. He left about an hour ago."

"Do you know where he went?"

"He went out with some friends. Where specifically, I'm not sure." She walked up the stairs until she was out of sight.

I wished I'd known it was his birthday today. He obviously didn't want me to know because he'd rather pretend it didn't exist, but he was my husband. I should know these things.

15

MAVERICK

"Not tonight, man." Kent slammed his hand down on the table. "Drinks are on me. I don't give a shit if you're a billionaire, birthday boys never buy their own drinks." He turned to the waitress who set the drinks in front of us. "Don't take his money, alright? His number is okay but no cash."

She addressed him but smiled at me. "Got it." She tucked her tray under her arm and walked away, her ass shaking in her tight skirt.

The guys were at the bar talking to two women they'd spotted the second they walked in, and since Kent and I weren't as hard up as the others, we took our time before we started the hunt. It was never smart to go after the first piece of ass you spotted. It was essential to figure out who had the nicest ass first.

"So, how's the wife?"

I had no idea what she was doing tonight, but since it was Saturday, I assumed she had a performance. "She's probably singing at the theatre." Kent knew the marriage was totally bogus, but he was still fascinated by the arrangement. "I haven't talked to her in a while."

"How does that work? You just don't see her for a couple of days?"

With one arm over the back of the booth, I drank the scotch, remembering the afternoon Arwen and I drank together. "It's a pretty big place. She sleeps on the second floor on one side of the house. I'm on the top floor on the opposite side."

"But you're fucking her, right?"

The only time I came close was on our wedding night. I didn't have much interest in her at the time, but when I thought she wanted me, I wasn't going to say no. That was purely for convenience, nothing else. "No."

"No?" Kent asked incredulously. "You're joking. You haven't fucked your own wife?"

"No." I took another drink.

He shook his head like he couldn't believe what I said. "Mav, not to be a dick, but she is gorgeous. On your wedding day, she was the sexiest woman there. She's probably the sexiest woman everywhere she goes."

I wasn't impressed as easily as he was, but I didn't deny that she was a looker. Ever since I'd been forced to marry her, my desire had been inhibited. She was a commitment I didn't want to have, not a sexy one-night stand I could kick out the next morning. She was an obligation...and that wasn't sexy. But as I'd gotten to know her over the last six weeks, I'd started to see her in a new way. She was a smart woman with incredible resilience. Sometimes she fell down...but she always picked herself up again. She'd garnered my respect...somehow.

"You can't sit there and tell me you disagree," Kent said. "It's just not possible."

"Yes...I think she's beautiful."

"Then why are you out drinking with me and the boys when you could be fucking her? Any piece of ass you pick up in here won't compare."

My relationship with Arwen had evolved since the night we'd met. There was an alliance between us, a partnership that was based on something akin to friendship. But she didn't want a physical relationship with me. She knew she could have me if she wanted me...based on our wedding night. Sometimes I caught glimpses of her looking at me, admiring my bare chest. When we kissed, I knew she could feel the heat between our lips. But perhaps that was just biology mixed with chemistry—nothing more. "That's not how our relationship is."

"What are you talking about? She's your wife."

"She doesn't want to sleep with me." I stared ahead and surveyed the people in the bar. It was my birthday, and I wanted to pretend it wasn't happening by drinking with the guys. I wanted to pretend I didn't care that my father forgot it was my birthday...and my sister didn't remember either. Birthdays were just countdowns until death, but I thought it would mean something to my own family. My mother wouldn't have forgotten.

"Are you sure about that?"

I nodded.

"Is she sleeping with other people?"

"We have an open relationship." I didn't care who she slept with, and she didn't care who I slept with. I just hoped she would open her legs to a man who actually deserved her, not more boys trying to be men. As I got to know her, I realized she deserved more than most people. She had a good heart and a beautifully proud spirit.

"Does that bother you?"

"No." My answer came out instantly.

"I don't know...if I had a wife who looked like that, I would be the only one allowed to fuck her."

I could control her if I wanted to. I could lock her up in the house and make her mine. I could strip away all her rights and turn her into a prisoner. I could threaten to kill any man she talked to, and when she got so horny she lost her mind, she would finally give in and fuck me. But I didn't want to be that guy. "I don't see her that way...as my wife. She's just a means to an end."

"And when are you finally going to cash in your reward?"

"Next week."

"Need any help?"

I shook my head. "No. This is personal—and we want to get our hands dirty." There would be torture followed by a gruesome death. I'd watch the entire thing, leaving my father to do the dirty work because it meant more to him. It would be grisly, but when it was over, we could wash our hands and move on.

THE BLONDE I was talking to was an easy mark. Her hand kept grabbing my thigh under the table, moving up until her fingers brushed the hard outline of my dick in my jeans. She made it clear she had no issues with getting right to the point.

Kent was beside me, talking to a brunette about the scars

on his hand. He traced them with his forefinger like he was mapping out the stars with all the cuts he'd received from his underground knife fights.

It was obvious when a pretty girl walked inside because all heads turned to the entryway. This one caught my attention in particular because every single person in the bar looked—the women included.

When she made her way past the congestion at the bar, she stepped farther inside, wearing a tight little black dress, black heels, and her hair was its own special production. With a small gift box tucked under her arm, she scanned the area like she was searching for someone.

I almost didn't recognize her. I'd seen her dress up before, but this dress had a dramatic slit up her thigh and a tightness around her chest that made her tits looked like fresh eggs on a platter. Her ass must have looked amazing because all the men behind her craned their necks to get a look at it.

The blonde kept talking and squeezing my thigh, oblivious to my otherwise-directed attention.

Arwen finally spotted me, and there was a slight joy that entered her gaze—like I was exactly who she was looking for. She headed to the table, her perfect figure moving flawlessly. Her hips shook from side to side, so womanly that they made me a bigger man on the spot.

Even Kent forgot about his girl when he noticed Arwen.

Arwen reached the table, unaffected by the woman who was sinking her claws into me. "Happy Birthday, Maverick."

The blonde moved closer to me, clearly not wanting to share.

I didn't understand so many things. How did she know it was my birthday? How did she know I was here? Why did she get me a present? I was speechless for a moment, my dick so hard it started to hurt inside my jeans—and it had nothing to do with the blonde.

Kent kicked me under the table, snapping me back to reality.

I dropped my arm from around the blonde. "Give us a couple minutes."

The blonde was clearly pissed. She looked at me like I'd just slapped her. "Someone else will snatch me up in a couple minutes." She slid out of the booth and marched off, angry she didn't get what she wanted.

Arwen immediately looked apologetic. "Sorry, I didn't mean to—"

"Sit down." I didn't want all the men in the bar to keep staring at her ass as she stood in front of my table.

She slid into the booth and placed the present in front of me. "It's not much, but I wanted you to have it."

I ignored it, looking at her with the same bewilderment. My arm moved over the back of the booth once more, subconsciously claiming her so the dogs would stop sniffing. When I glanced at her left hand, I noticed the princess cut diamond ring I gave her, shining more brilliantly than any other piece of jewelry anyone else wore. "What are you doing here?"

"Liam told me you were celebrating your birthday here with friends... I thought I was also a friend." Her attitude slipped into her tone, offended that I wasn't touched by the gesture.

I didn't see her as a friend—but I didn't tell her that. "How did you know it was my birthday?"

"How about you stop asking a million questions and just

open your present?" She sat up straight with her arms on the table, the curve in her back so deep that it made her ass look even bigger.

I stared at her, slightly embarrassed she was there, but I was even more embarrassed because I was touched by the gift.

Kent watched us. "Asshole, your wife got you a birthday present. Put a smile on your face and open it." He slid out of the booth with the girl he'd been flirting with. They traveled to the bar to get another drink.

Leaving me alone with her.

She kept watching me, and when I didn't open it, her eyes started to fill with sadness. "I finished at the theater, and I wanted to stop by and give this to you. I didn't mean to embarrass you or ruin—"

"You just caught me off guard. That's all." And I never let anyone catch me off guard. I grabbed the present and ripped through the wrapping, revealing a picture frame. It was a photo of my mother and me. It had been taken on Easter Sunday. She was in a white dress with her fingernails painted in pastels. I wore a collared shirt she'd gotten me for my birthday. It was the last holiday we'd celebrated before she died. My hand started to shake as I held the picture, remembering that spring day so perfectly.

"I noticed you don't have any picture frames on your desk... I thought you could put this up. Abigail found the picture for me."

The only reason Abigail helped her was because she liked her...and she wanted me to lighten up.

Arwen kept watching me as I stared at the picture.

It was difficult to pull my gaze away because I wished my

mother were still here. I wished I could put the frame down, then look up and see her face. My heart had hardened into stone, so I hardly ever felt anything...but this made me feel so much. When I couldn't look at it anymore, I turned the picture over onto the table. "Thank you..." I still hadn't looked at Arwen yet, unsure what to say to her. She'd just chased away an easy lay, but I couldn't care less about getting pussy anymore.

She pulled the picture back toward her. "I'll take it back to the house for you. I thought I could hang out with your friends, but it looks like you guys are all doing the same thing..." Picking up women to take home.

"How did you know it was my birthday?"

"I caught Abigail sneaking a cupcake to your room."

She did it every year—even though I asked her not to. "I'm pretty tired. I think I'm ready to head home."

"I didn't mean to scare off your date."

"If I really wanted to take someone home, I would make it happen." Now the idea of taking home a random woman felt anticlimactic. I didn't feel the angry bitterness in my chest anymore. Now there was warmth there...so I didn't want something meaningless.

"Alright." She rolled up the wrapping paper and grabbed the picture frame. "I guess I'll see you at the house." She slid out of the booth and rose to her feet.

Once again, every man in the room turned to gawk at her, to check out her perfect legs, petite waist, and sexy-as-fuck tits.

I didn't like it.

I got to my feet and circled my arm around her waist.

She flinched at the touch but brushed it off just as quickly.

When we walked out, I saw the blonde give me the coldest stare. She felt replaced by a woman so beautiful she couldn't possibly compete. Kent winked at me from the bar then gave me a thumbs-up, telling me to go for it.

We left the bar, and I walked her to her Mercedes a few blocks away at the curb. I didn't want her walking around dressed like that. I was surprised she made it to the bar without being accosted by ten different guys.

I opened the door for her.

"Wow, I didn't know you had manners."

I looked down at her, realizing how short she was even in heels. I towered over her so easily, getting a perfect view of her bustiness. "It's rare, but it happens."

WE RETURNED to the house and walked into the entryway.

She had the picture frame tucked under her arm, her long hair cascading around her shoulders. She smelled so good, like a field of flowers. When she performed at the opera, she didn't work up a sweat, even though her vocal cords were commanded to do the extraordinary. She even went to a bar afterward, not wiped out by the exertion it must have taken.

She gripped the rail and climbed up the staircase, her feet still in the five-inch heels.

I walked beside her, more aware of her attractiveness than ever before. Kent didn't need to point it out to me because I always knew she was beautiful. I just never entertained the idea because there was so much resentment in the way.

We reached the second floor, and she extended the picture frame to me. "If you don't want to put up the picture, it's no big deal—"

"No, it should go up. I just have to decide where." I glanced at it and held it at my side. If she'd gotten me something else, like a shirt or a watch, I probably would have been a dick to her. The night would have gone quite differently. But when I realized how sentimental the gift was, I didn't have an angry bone in my body.

She gave a slight smile. "I was afraid you would get mad… It seems like you're always mad."

In her defense, she was right. I was usually brooding over something. Sometimes I was stressed about work, sometimes I was thinking about how much I hated my father, and sometimes I remembered all the terrible things that had happened to my mother. It was enough to make anyone angry all the time. "I am always angry."

"Well…I hope you had a good birthday." She turned her body slightly, like she was about to walk ahead and go into her bedroom.

"I did. But there's something else I want for my birthday." Before I knew what I was saying, the words were out of my mouth and in the air. Maybe I'd drunk too much scotch, or maybe I thought I had a real chance because of the thoughtful gift she'd just given me. Or maybe she just looked so damn hot, I wanted to lift up her dress and fuck her right up against the wall.

She stiffened in place, like she knew exactly what I meant. Her eyes focused on my face, and her breathing changed. Her tits firmed against her dress, her nipples piercing through the thin material. She could have turned away and brushed off the comment, but she continued to linger.

I stepped closer to her, my lips aching for those full and delicious lips of hers. My imagination skipped ahead and pictured our naked bodies on my bed, her hard nipples being sucked raw by my anxious mouth. I opened her legs and tasted her there too, seeing if she was sweet or sour. Then I finally got my dick inside her—and fucked my wife.

She didn't step back, but her lips parted slightly.

My hand slid into her hair, and I cradled her face so I could take her mouth. I moved closer and felt my dick nearly break through my zipper. With my arms locked behind her knees, I pictured myself sinking deep inside her tight little pussy. I imagined being buried to the hilt, taking this gorgeous woman who every man dreamed of fucking.

My fingers tightened in her hair, and I rested my mouth closer to hers, feeling the anticipation heighten just before the kiss. I'd kissed her before, but it was an obligation, a performance. This was the first time I truly wanted her, not just because she was offering herself. I desired her like a man desired his fantasy.

My arm wrapped around her waist, and I brought her into me as I kissed her.

Fuck.

I felt her soft lips as a shiver ran down my spine. Smooth and slightly wet, they tasted like scotch and lipstick. I pulled her breath out of her lungs and into mine as I kissed her, claimed her mouth as my property. My fingers tightened a little more as I tilted my head and deepened the kiss.

Her lips moved with mine, shy at first, but then aggressive

and sexy. She took a breath as she felt me, her hands moving to my stomach so she could feel my abs through my shirt. She pressed hard into me as I flexed for her, letting her feel what a real man felt like. A tiny moan escaped her lips, so small it could barely be heard.

Maybe I imagined it.

I imagined her soaked panties. I imagined fingering her pussy and getting my fingers coated in her arousal. I imagined staring at her sexy asshole as I fucked her from behind. I imagined heart-pounding, dirty, dirty sex.

Her hands migrated up my stomach to my chest, studying the grooves and muscle of my frame. When she got to my shoulders, she squeezed them with her slender fingers then cupped my face, feeling the friction of my facial hair as she touched my chin.

My hand covered both of her ass cheeks, and I squeezed.

She was a sexy kisser.

I had another floor to go before we reached my bedroom, but I had condoms in my pocket, so I would fuck her in her room. I started to back her up and guide her to the first flat surface I could get her to.

But she stopped kissing me instead.

She pulled away with her hand resting on my arms, her eyes downcast as she avoided my gaze by looking at my chest. Her lips were still parted, and she breathed deep and hard because that kiss knocked the wind out of her like it did me. Then her fingertips touched her bottom lip, like the electricity between us had numbed her mouth in the process. "Goodnight..." She pulled away and walked into her bedroom.

I watched her go with a hard dick in my pants. The

second I tried to take it further, it spooked her. I was tempted to go after her, to press her head into the mattress and force her ass in the air so I could take her anyway. I'd never been overcome with such an urge to take a woman violently. This was my house, and she was my property. I could do whatever the fuck I wanted.

But before I did anything rash, I breathed through the pounding arousal in my dick and calmed myself. I could make this happen if I wanted to, but it would go against my promise. I'd vowed to protect her and take care of her.

Not force her to fuck me.

Even though my hands were balled into fists and my rage circulated in my blood, I turned around and went to bed.

16

ARWEN

I ALMOST DID SOMETHING REALLY STUPID LAST NIGHT.

I almost slept with my husband.

When he kissed me, I knew I should have pulled away... but I didn't. Once his lips were on mine and I felt that incredible body with my fingertips, I got lost in the lust. I pictured myself on my back while that beautiful man fucked me until I came around his dick.

But that was a terrible idea.

I could barely tolerate the man when things weren't complicated. What would happen once we started sleeping together? Would it be just a one-time thing? Or would it cause problems? Maverick and I weren't in a monogamous relationship, so we were more like coworkers. You don't shit where you eat.

If this was a lifelong commitment, I couldn't see us casually sleeping together without consequences.

I didn't see Maverick for a few days because I spent a lot of time at the theater...and I was purposely avoiding him. He seemed to be busy with work anyway, so we didn't cross paths. Soon he would be taking out Ramon, so that might keep him busy for a few days.

But eventually, I would have to face him.

I wasn't the kind of person to shy away from conflict, but I was dreading this conversation with Maverick. He wasn't much of a talker, so he might pretend it never happened, choosing to be a passive-aggressive asshole.

Not that that was much better.

When I came home from the theatre, the moment arrived. I stepped inside the house and found him standing in the entryway, sorting through his mail while wearing a black suit. His powerful physique filled out the garment so well, making it fit him like a glove. He hardly ever wore suits, so he must have had serious business that afternoon.

There was no way around him without getting his attention, so I sucked it up and moved to the stairs.

He didn't look up from the letter he was reading. "How long are you going to drag this out?" He flipped to another envelope and checked it before moving on to the next. He didn't bother to look up and read my reaction. He seemed to feel it.

I slowly turned back to him, knowing he was right. I couldn't be a coward forever. "Until now, I guess."

He tossed the envelopes onto the center table, which held a massive sculpture that rose toward the chandelier hanging from the high, vaulted ceiling. His dark eyes showed his irritation. He wasn't the gentle man he'd been a few nights ago on his birthday. He'd reverted back to the asshole he was before. "If you don't want to fuck me, don't lead me on. You've done it twice now."

My jaw almost dropped to the floor. "I did not lead you on—"

"You follow me to a bar on my birthday, dressed like you're trying to torture me, and then you give me a photograph of my mother?" He tilted his head as he examined me with cold eyes. "Don't backpedal. That's exactly what you did."

"I'm not backpedaling. I was being a friend. That's what we are, right? Maybe you've never had a relationship with a woman that wasn't straight sex, but that was me being more than just a quick fuck."

He still looked pissed. "I would have preferred the fuck."

I rolled my eyes. "You're a pig."

"I'm a man." He stepped toward me, crowding me into the banister of the stairs. "I'm a man who likes to fuck beautiful women. If you don't want to be one of those women, then stop with the bullshit. Just stay out of my way and pretend you don't exist."

"So, it's one or the other?" I asked incredulously. "I either sleep with you or live under a rock?"

"That's a good way to put it."

I wanted to slap him again. "I didn't sleep with you because it would complicate things. Would it be a one-time thing? Would we forget it ever happened? Would we keep doing it? Would we continue to see other people? It's just easier if we don't go down that road."

"You are my wife. Husbands are supposed to fuck their wives. You're overthinking it."

"So just casually?" I asked.

"Yes. You were fucking Dante casually. How is that any different?"

I didn't want to talk about the man who dumped me. "Leave him out of this."

"You told me you were going to have lovers. Why can't I be one of those lovers?"

Maverick wasn't like the men I took to bed. He was more handsome than all of them combined, but he was also a huge dick. Sometimes he was kind, but sometimes he was equally cruel. "Because I don't like you."

His eyes fell, as if the words actually hurt him.

"You're nice to me once in a while and then a dick to me ten seconds later. Like right now, you're a completely different guy than the last time we were together. Our relationship is already complicated enough. Add fucking into the mix, and it's gonna be a shitshow."

He kept staring at me with eyes as strong as espresso. "It's not complicated—you're what's complicated. We could fuck like every other man and woman out there, no strings attached. Sometimes we screw, sometimes we don't. No big deal."

"It never works that way. Every man I've ever been with always wants more."

His eyes narrowed before a sarcastic laugh exploded from his mouth. "You won't have that problem with me. The only reason I want to fuck you is because of the way you look in a tight dress. That's all I'm ever going to want from you—so get over yourself."

Now I really did want to slap him so hard his cheek would be red for a week. "I'm just telling you—"

"You're the one who's going to want to fuck me. I see the way you look at me, I feel the way you kiss me. You'll get sick of boys like Dante and want to be fucked by a real man. Don't wait too long...because I might lose interest."

"Wow...you're the one who needs to get over yourself."

He grabbed the stack of mail from the table and tucked it under his arm. "Stay out of my way." He moved toward me as he approached the stairs, his shoulder coming close to mine. "I mean it."

"You weren't kidding when you said I would change my mind." I turned and watched him reach the first step of the large staircase.

He stopped his progression but didn't turn around to look at me.

"You were right. I do hate you."

AN ENTIRE WEEK PASSED, and I did what he asked—stayed out of his way.

I had breakfast in my room, went to the gym when I knew he was finished with his workout, and I minded my own business.

It got lonely after a while.

He had a large swimming pool with a beautiful deck that overlooked his property, so I spent time in the sun while reading. When it got too hot, I dipped in the water for a cooldown. Having servants that would refresh my drink and bring cheese platters and bowls of fruit was a dream come true.

But I still felt empty inside.

Now that Dante was gone and my father was dead, I felt like the only person on the planet. I didn't realize how much I talked to Maverick until that bridge had been burned. We'd had a great night together at the bar for his birthday. He seemed to like the present I got him. But things went south... and now our friendship was gone too.

I couldn't live like this forever. I couldn't be at war with my only ally.

But I didn't want to sleep with him to make peace.

It would make me feel like a whore.

It would be a lie to say the thought didn't cross my mind. When we kissed at the top of the stairs, my lips were so hot, they felt like they were on fire. My lungs inhaled as much air as possible because kissing him was just so damn good.

A man had never kissed me like that before.

If he kissed that well, I imagined he could do everything else just as well.

Maybe his ego really did come from somewhere.

I was sitting in my room alone watching TV when I started to think about Maverick. Distance made the heart grow fonder, and I began to despise him less. I remembered how good he was to me during my darkest days. He held me at our wedding so I could shed a few tears for my dying father. He gripped my hand at the funeral. He comforted me when I sat in the darkness and wished I were dead. He was such a bastard...but he could be a good man too.

He wasn't my enemy.

He was my ally.

I had no idea if he was home, but at this hour, he would be in his office or bedroom. Dinner would have finished an hour ago, so there was nowhere else he could be. I took the stairs to the third floor and approached his bedroom door, knowing I would be greeted with a demonic threat. Maverick could be the most intimidating man on the planet if you got on his bad side. That ice-cold expression would be on his face, those coffee-colored eyes full of hatred. He would probably insult me a couple of times before I could even get a single word in. He might even slam the door in my face.

I raised my fist to knock on the door, but I stopped when I heard what he was doing.

"Maverick..." A woman's sexy voice filled the room with a moan. The sound of the creaking bed was audible a second later, along with the tap of the headboard against the wall. His pace was quick, like he was dominating that mattress, like he was conquering her. The woman's breathing was so loud, I could hear it through the closed door. She panted louder and harder, like she was just seconds away from coming.

I should have walked away in revulsion, but I stayed. Like a creeper, I kept listening through the door, imagining how that fit man looked naked. He seemed like he was rocking her world, and now I couldn't stop picturing it in my head. How was he fucking her? Was he on top doing all the work? Was she riding his dick up and down? Was he as big as his ego suggested?

I should leave now and stop wondering.

But I stayed. I wanted to hear him moan, hear him come. I wanted to hear him enjoy himself so I could add it to my imagination. I was attracted to him when we kissed, but now I realized how deep that lust ran.

Why else would I still be standing there?

I took it a step further and cracked open the door. My eye focused on the tiny slit I'd made, and I could see them fucking on his bed. Just as I imagined, he was on top. He had a blond woman underneath him, his muscular arms were pinned behind her knees, and he was pounding her like a man with the endurance of a racehorse. He kept giving her his entire length, hitting her until he was balls deep inside her.

Now I realized he really did have something to be arrogant about...

His chiseled body looked even sexier with a sheen of sweat, of exertion that showed how hard he pushed his body. His shoulders were more powerful bare, and his stomach tightened even further every time he thrust. With muscular legs and a tight ass, he looked like a moving sculpture. His eyes were trained on the beautiful blonde underneath, watching her tits shake up and down as he kept her in a tight ball, fucking her into the mattress as she came.

Now I couldn't stop watching.

Her toes curled as her head rolled back, incoherent moans rising to the high ceiling. Her nails clawed at his chest, sliding past the sweat and muscle. "Yes...fuck...yes." She arched her back, and her nipples hardened as if every single cell in her body felt the powerful pleasure.

Maverick kept going as if he wasn't finished. The woman had clearly gotten her fix, but he wanted to keep fucking her anyway. Keeping his load in check so he could keep going, he continued to fuck the woman like he could last all night.

She moaned like she knew this stud would keep pleasing her.

It was time to shut the door and walk away. I'd violated his privacy enough. I shouldn't even have come to his bedroom at this time of night, knowing what he usually did up here.

I felt the heat in my cheeks, the urge to linger until he

finished. I wanted to see how he looked when he came, if he was still the ferocious asshole I encountered on a daily basis. Or did he soften just a bit? Did he give in to the passion and let his guard down? Did he look even more handsome when he filled the tip of the condom?

I wanted to find out, but the last thing I needed was to get caught.

He might break his promise and hurt me.

I closed the door gently and could still hear them fucking like dogs. The heat rushed up my body and made my fingertips go numb. My lips felt so lonely, as if Maverick's kiss was the only thing that would make me feel complete.

I forced myself down the hallway and remembered how good his kiss felt, remembered being in those powerful arms as his big hands gripped me. I remembered how petite I felt when he grabbed my ass like it was a piece of meat. He was such a good kisser...the best I'd ever had.

Now I wondered if he was the best fuck I'd ever have.

17

MAVERICK

My father had all the schematics on the table, showing the exact spot where we would be once the mission was launched. Bottles of brandy were everywhere, most of them empty. Burned-out cigars were sprinkled like decorations. Once my mother died, he stopped giving a damn about his health.

I'd never cared about mine.

With a cigar in his mouth, he made the notes on the table. "You'll be here with your men." He marked it with a red X. "I'll come in from the side. Even if he's more armed than we anticipate, he'll have a battle on two fronts. We'll kill all his men, take whatever artillery that can be salvaged, and capture him alive." It was the only time my father had been calm in a year. He spoke about the plan in a bored voice, like this wasn't as climactic as getting the information in the first place. "We'll keep him in the barn at the center of your property."

I had dairy cows in the pasture, their prized milk used for producing cheese. There was a barn out there, far away from the other buildings so the smell of shit wouldn't reach my nose when I fucked a woman in my pool. "But not for long, right?"

He puffed his cigar and let the smoke rise to the ceiling. "We'll see what my mood is like…"

I'd expected him to keep Ramon on his own property, but perhaps that was too disturbing for him—to have the man who raped his wife in his home.

"Any questions?"

"No."

My father studied me, letting small wisps of smoke escape from his parted lips. He watched me for a long time, as if he were having a conversation with me inside his head. "We can't afford any mistakes. Do you understand?"

I wouldn't make any mistakes. "Yes."

"I'm counting on you, Maverick. Fuck it up, and I'll never forgive you." He puffed his cigar again.

I wanted to press the hot ash directly into his neck and make him scream. "You won't kill me?" I couldn't keep the edge out of my voice. "That's a step up…"

He put out the cigar in the black ashtray. "They say disappointing your father is the worst punishment a son can feel."

I'd been nothing but a disappointment to him for the past year, and it certainly did feel like a punishment. I wanted to rise to my feet and slam a bottle of brandy over his head, but I convinced myself this was the end of his malice. Once he got what he wanted, he would have closure…and that closure would kill this dark spirit that had taken over his body. He would feel human again…and be a father again. "That's debatable."

I HADN'T SEEN Arwen in a week.

When I told her to stay out of my way, she listened.

She didn't show her face during meals, and she didn't cross my path when I came and went. It seemed like she'd taken my threat seriously. Sometimes I forgot she lived there altogether...and that was a gift.

She'd rejected me twice—and now I was done.

If she didn't want to fuck me, that was one thing. But she teased me. She kissed me and liked it. She touched my stomach like she wanted to unbutton my shirt and slide it down my arms so she could see what she'd just touched. She felt the same chemistry, felt the same desire. We would live in this house together until one of us died.

And she didn't plan on fucking me even once?

That seemed unlikely.

Eventually, she would cave. She would open her legs and ask me to fuck her—and I would turn her down.

See how she liked it.

I stopped at the table in the entryway and saw the pile of mail that needed to be sorted. Most of it was bullshit, paper that shouldn't have been used in the first place. Too tired after meeting with my father, I decided to deal with it tomorrow and headed up the stairs.

I'd been thinking about our plan so deeply I almost didn't notice Arwen standing there.

In a purple dress with one strap that crossed her shoulder, she had her hair and makeup done like she was off for a night at the opera. Her eyelashes were so thick, just as they were the last time I kissed her. Her makeup was applied so well, it almost looked natural—even though it was stage makeup. The strange thing about Arwen was how good she looked with or without makeup. She looked amazing, no matter what.

I had no idea what she wanted, but the second she spoke, something stupid would come out of her mouth. Just looking at her pissed me off. She'd teased me too many times now, and I just wanted her to disappear. Marrying her had sucked in the beginning—but now it was unbearable. I gave her a cold look before I kept walking.

"Maverick."

I ignored her and rounded the landing so I could move up the next flight of stairs. When I hadn't detested her so much, I'd given her my attention when she asked for it. When she'd needed a friend, I'd been there for her. When she'd needed a shoulder to cry on during her father's funeral, I'd been there for her.

But now I wasn't there for her anymore.

I could hear her footsteps behind me. She wore heels, and they gently echoed against the rug that covered the hardwood floor.

I kept going, refusing to give her the time of day. Tomorrow night, I was finally getting vengeance for my mother. I wouldn't let Ramon slip through my fingers—and I would kill every man who tried to protect him. I didn't have time for whatever bullshit she wanted to throw at me.

"Maverick."

I headed to my bedroom, prepared to slam the door in her face.

"Would you just talk to me?"

I turned around when I was on the threshold. "No." Her

beauty had no effect on me, not like it did on everyone else. I'd given in to her looks because I'd had too many drinks in my system, but now I had a clear head. I'd been getting pussy every night, so my dick wasn't hard up anymore. I turned back into my room and shut the door.

She caught the edge and pushed it open again. "Abigail told me you were at your father's."

I slowly turned around, my eyes narrowing. "Anything she doesn't tell you?" It was so damn humid this evening, the heat was suffocating. Indifferent to her presence, I pulled my shirt over my head and tossed it on one of the armchairs, knowing Abigail would pick it up tomorrow when I went to work.

Her gaze immediately went to my chest, her eyes showing a brief instant of vulnerability.

I wasn't falling for that shit again.

She forced her eyes back to mine. "Are you going to kill that man? The one who hurt your mother?" She stepped farther into my room, inviting herself inside even though she wasn't welcome. The last time she was there was on our wedding night—and she asked me to take off her dress.

When she asked about my family, I had a hard time ignoring her. Despite the hatred between us, she seemed to care about my grief. She wouldn't have given me that picture if she didn't understand how much my mother meant to me. "We're going to capture him tomorrow night."

"Tomorrow?" she whispered, a tone of surprise in her voice.

"Yes." I sat in the chair and took off my shoes and socks, doing my nightly routine like she wasn't there. I left them on the ground then stood again, ready to take off my jeans the second she got out of my face.

"Will it be dangerous?"

I respected this woman because she had beauty and brains—but right now, she had neither. "Obviously."

"Will you be alright?"

"Your guess is as good as mine."

She tilted her head slightly, the frustration in her eyes. "You should give your mother the vengeance she deserves, but she wouldn't want you to risk your life for her. I never met her, but I can tell you she would want you to walk away if there was any chance you could get hurt."

Yes, that was exactly what she would say. "Doesn't change anything. Now, get out." I'd almost gone to the bar to pick up a woman for the night, but I'd skipped it because I was too tired. Now I wished I had someone—just to get rid of Arwen.

Like the annoying little pest she was, she stayed. With her large eyes, she looked at me as if she wanted to say something, but the words wouldn't leave her full lips. With only one strap to her dress, her other shoulder was bare. Just like her face, her shoulder had the most beautiful complexion, skin that looked as soft as a rose petal.

The longer she stayed, the more annoyed I became. "Get. The. Fuck. Out." I stepped toward her, attempting to intimidate her with my size. I always had to kick women out of my room, but I'd never had to force someone like this. Sometimes I had to be an asshole to get what I wanted, but I never had to be *such* an asshole.

She stood her ground. "I'm worried about you."

"Well, don't be." I didn't need this woman to care about me like a real wife. She was just leeching off my protection, using me to keep psychopaths like Kamikaze away. I was tempted to tell her that a monster wanted her to sell pussy for cash, but I wasn't *that* much of an asshole.

She looked up at me through those thick eyelashes, her eyes even more alluring with all the dark makeup surrounding them. Her dress wasn't as revealing as the one she wore last week, but it still hugged her womanly curves in all the right places. With perky tits, a slender waist, and an ass so high, it seemed like she did squats every day, she had the kind of body a man was meant to grab on to.

"You don't care whether I live or die. So, cut the shit."

Hostility entered her expression. "That's not true, and you know it—"

"Last week, you said you didn't like me."

"I meant that in a romantic way. I didn't want to sleep with you because I don't see you like that—"

"You know I wasn't looking for romance. I never look for romance. I look for good sex—exclusively." I stepped closer to her, hoping she would eventually give in and take a step back. But she stood her ground, letting our faces come so close to each other. "You don't care about me, and that's okay. Because I don't care about you." My eyes shifted back and forth as I looked into hers, seeing the insult slowly enter her gaze then fester. I wanted to hurt this woman so she would leave me alone. It'd been a long day—and I'd smoked and drunk way too much. When I made my point, I turned away.

She grabbed me by the arm, her slender fingers digging into my skin. Her grip was feisty, as if she was prepared to fight me in order to keep my attention. She yanked on my limb and pulled me back to her.

The only reason it worked was because I allowed it to

happen. I turned back to her, prepared to yell in her face and strip her down to tears. The past week had been peaceful because she'd removed herself from my existence. But now she was grabbing me, like she somehow owned me.

Before I could say a word, she moved into me and planted her lips on mine, two soft clouds pressing against my scotch-soaked lips. Her fingers gripped me a little tighter once our lips came together, fitting perfectly just like last time.

The fight left my veins, all the insults dropping from my mind. Once I tasted a woman, I abandoned all thoughts of the outside world. All I focused on was the smell of her hair, the softness of her skin. I'd kissed this woman before, and it was just as good as last time—even better because she was the one who'd kissed me.

Was that the reason she'd come here tonight?

When she knew I wouldn't slip away, her fingers relaxed on my arm and she kept kissing me, her lips more aggressive than last time. She breathed into my mouth as she caressed my bottom lip, her lips wet from the kiss.

I kissed her a little harder, my body finally humming to life when I realized this was real. My hand moved to her neck, and my fingers dug under the fall of her hair. When my arm wrapped around her petite waistline, she moaned into my mouth.

I guided her backward, gently pressing her into the wall next to the door. My mouth took hers harder, and I slipped my tongue into her mouth for the first time. Heat burned in my blood when I felt her small tongue greet mine, just as anxious.

My hand bunched up her dress, making it rise up her thighs until it reached her waist. She didn't pull away when it got too intimate, not like last time. My fingers kept gripping, pulling it higher up until it gathered around her waist.

She kissed me harder, her mouth begging mine for more. When she rubbed her tongue against mine, she made the sexiest sigh, hitting a musical note that resonated in my soul. Her hands explored my shoulders, feeling all the individual muscles before she slid them down over my chest, pressing her palms into my body like she wanted to test just how hard I really was.

I could show her instead.

I gripped the back of her knee and lifted her leg against my hip, wrapping her leg around my waist as I pinned her against the wall. My dick was hard in my jeans, the tip reaching the waistband of my pants. I pressed into her perfectly, my shaft giving her clit the ideal pressure to make her hips buck automatically.

She moaned against my mouth, her eyelids lifting slowly so she could look at my eyes. Her hands latched on to my arms for balance, and she was so far gone with lust that she was a whole different woman. Her lips parted, and she breathed as she felt every single inch of my hard dick.

Now I wondered if she was as good in bed as she claimed.

She rested her head against mine, her eyes downcast as she felt me grind against her. As if she'd never felt a dick so big and so hard, she was unable to do anything other than enjoy the pleasure screaming from her clit. Her nails started to dig into me because she was so anxious. If my dick felt this good through jeans and underwear, it would feel a million times better inside her.

Her hand cupped the side of my face, and she pulled me in for a kiss, her mouth even more aggressive this time. She slowly rocked her hips into me like we were fucking against the wall. She got herself off on the hardness of my cock, the fullness of my lips. Her fingers cupped the back of my head, and she kissed me like I wasn't just some lay for the night. She kissed me like I was the man she was hopelessly in love with.

She was good.

With her lips still kissing mine, she moved her hand to my jeans and slipped the button loose. Her fingers grabbed the zipper and started to pull it down, letting my bulge press through my boxers a little more. She pushed my jeans down and then reached for my boxers, prepared to get them off so we could fuck right here against the wall.

I stepped back and pulled my jeans up.

Her leg dropped and her hands returned to her sides when she had nothing left to grab on to. A look of bewilderment and rage started to creep into her features and erase the lust that glowed in her eyes.

I zipped up my jeans and fastened the button. "Get out."

"You can't be this spiteful."

I opened the bedroom door. "I am." I stood with my hand on the doorframe, waiting for her to pull her dress down and walk out of the room. I could have glanced down and looked at her sexy legs and the black thong that barely covered anything, but I kept my dark eyes focused on her horrified face.

When she realized that this was really happening, that she was getting a bitter taste of her own medicine, she slowly pulled her dress down, licked her lips like there was a drop of scotch in the corner of her mouth, and held her head high as she walked out of my bedroom.

Before I shut the door, I gave her another livid stare. "Not so fun, is it?"

She turned around, her eyes narrowed like she wanted to grab my neck and strangle me.

I slammed the door in her face.

18

ARWEN

I SAT ON THE COUCH IN MY BEDROOM, STILL EMBARRASSED FROM the night before. When I went to his room, my heart was full of concern for his departure. He was about to embark on a dangerous journey for vengeance, the very thing his marriage to me had purchased. But anytime there was warfare, there were casualties.

I didn't want him to be one of those casualties.

He was a difficult man who was spiteful and rude, but he had good qualities...when he chose to show them. There were lots of times that he'd been good to me when he didn't have to. It made me forgive his flaws and appreciate his kindness. That meant I didn't want him to die...especially when he was trying to do the right thing for his mother.

And if he died, what would happen to me? I would be broke, homeless, and unprotected.

I needed him.

There wasn't a knock on my door before he stepped inside. He usually respected my space, but after things went south, he seemed to hate me.

"Do you mind?" I stood up and faced him. "I could have been naked."

"Wouldn't have made a difference to me." He tossed a small bag on the coffee table. It made a noticeable thud when it hit the wood. "I'm leaving in a few hours. Wanted you to have this."

"What?" It was hard to look at him and not think about my back against the wall, my clit throbbing against his big dick. When my leg was anchored around his waist and our lips were locked together, I forgot who we were. In that moment, we were just a man and a woman. My panties had been soaked when I'd returned to my bedroom, and while I was humiliated by the way he rejected me, I'd still touched myself before I went to sleep.

Maverick was still hostile, like his vengeance hadn't been enough for him. "Cash. Fake IDs and passports."

I glanced at the cloth bag before I turned back to him. "And why do I need those?"

"In case I don't come back." He pulled a pistol out of his back pocket and handed it to me. "Know how to use this?"

I'd never held a gun in my life. "No."

He showed me the safety before he set it down. "It's loaded. Be careful."

I didn't want to live in a reality where I needed it. "You could just not leave and take the gun back."

"I have to do this." He was in jeans and a t-shirt like it was an ordinary day. It didn't seem as though he would disappear into the night and kill his biggest enemy. His hard body stretched his clothes as they had the other night. It was hard to look at him and not picture him shirtless. "Even if I knew I was going to die, I would do it anyway."

"I hope not..."

"She would do it for me." He came closer to me, speaking to me like someone could be eavesdropping. "If I don't make it back, take a car and disappear. These IDs should last you for a while. There's enough cash for you to start over. But lay low—because people will be looking for you."

"Please come back..." I didn't realize how much I needed him until I was forced to think about my life without him. So far, I'd never felt insecure or afraid. He gave me everything I needed, took care of me the way my father took care of me. He'd become the foundation I'd built my new life on. I hated being here, but now I realized I really had no other choice. "Not just because I need you...but because I want you to come back."

He watched me with unmoving eyes. His stare was so focused, it almost seemed like he didn't hear what I said. "I'll come back. A wolf won't leave his sheep unprotected for long." He moved back slightly.

"I thought the wolf ate the sheep...?" I crossed my arms over my chest, fear in my heart.

"I guess I'm not hungry yet." He turned away and headed to the door.

I stared at his strong back, the muscles stretching his shirt in different places. It was almost seven in the evening, and the light was disappearing from the horizon. My stomach was full from dinner, and while I lived in a comfortable fortress where no one could bother me, I suddenly felt alone. I only had one man in my life—and he was leaving. "Maverick?"

Unlike last night, he actually stopped. He slowly turned around and looked at me, giving me the opportunity to say what was on my mind. But the offer was fleeting. He didn't have the patience to wait long, especially when he was annoyed with me.

I came close to him, my fingers possessing the memory of his hard jaw. My lips still felt his. I could even imagine his hard dick against me. I did last night when my fingers were between my legs. But my attraction faded into the background when I was faced with the harsh reality of his absence. He was about to leave me—and he may not come back. I moved into his torso and wrapped my arms around his waist. My cheek found a home against his hard chest, and I closed my eyes, never wanting to let go. It was the first hug I'd ever given him, and the affection felt right. My feelings for him were so contradictory, like we were two survivors stranded on an island. We didn't like each other, but we had to put aside our differences if we wanted to live.

He didn't hug me back. His arms stayed by his sides as he allowed me to touch him.

"Please be careful…" I respected and hated this man at the same time. There were some days when I hated him more than liked him, but then the very next day, it would be the exact opposite. Every day was an adventure. But right now, I knew I wanted him to come back in one piece.

I released my grip and turned away, accepting his coldness without insult. He'd never been an affectionate man, and he wouldn't start now. All he wanted from me was sex and obedience. Since I couldn't provide either, I was worthless to him.

His hand grabbed my arm, and he yanked me back into him. One hand slid into my hair, while the other gripped the small of my back, squeezing the fabric in his fingertips so it rose up my thighs. Before I could process what was happening, his mouth was on mine. He kissed me just the way he had last night, like no time had passed at all. We picked up where we left off, our tongues sliding together as we exchanged breaths. His hand gently yanked on my hair, controlling the tilt of my head the way he controlled the arch in my back. His full lips moved with mine, opening, closing, filling me with his masculine energy.

My hands glided up his shirt and explored my favorite part of his body. My fingers played with the grooves of his abs, brushing against warm concrete before I stroked them up his chest, feeling the hard planes of strength. His skin was so warm to the touch, his muscles so hard. I'd never touched a stronger man. He made my former lovers seem soft by comparison.

He suddenly pulled away, ending the kiss and taking his affection with him.

"No..." I abandoned my pride and moved into him again, my nails clawing into his skin so he couldn't get away. My mouth claimed his as he'd claimed mine just seconds ago. "Come on...please." I didn't realize how much I wanted this man until I couldn't have him, until I'd had a taste. Watching him fuck that woman in his bed made me want to be fucked just as hard. I was so lonely in this castle, in this empty world. The only somewhat meaningful relationship I had was with my husband...so I wanted him between my legs. I wanted him to chase away the loneliness, to make me feel safe.

He pulled away again, an arrogant grin on that handsome face. He pushed the door closed without taking his eyes off me. "Just wanted to get the door."

"Oh..." Embarrassment flooded through me when I realized how much I'd just begged this man to stay with me. It was instinct...whispering the word please. He'd hung me out to dry last night, and I couldn't go through it again, not when I already knew how extraordinary the sex would be.

He came back to me and brought his lips close to mine. "Looks like I've punished you enough." His hand returned to my hair, and he kissed me again, dominating the embrace by taking the lead. As he backed me up to the bed, he lifted my dress up my thighs until it was bunched around my waist. His fingers slid over my bare ass and hooked around my thong, playing with it as he kissed me while still holding a handful of hair.

I'd never wanted a man more in my life.

My fingers found the hem of his shirt, and they trembled as I pulled the material over his head. Now I knew this would really happen, that he wouldn't pull away and leave me hanging again. His punishment taught me how much I wanted him, that I shouldn't throw away another opportunity. I didn't know what this meant for us, but it didn't seem to matter. Whether this was a one-time thing or the beginning of an unspoken relationship, it didn't matter. There was no way I could live under his roof for the rest of my life without giving in once in a while. Besides, tonight could be his last night on this earth. If it didn't happen now, it might never happen.

My fingers got his jeans loose, and I pushed them down until they fell around his ankles.

He gripped the material of my dress and pulled it over my head, revealing my figure in just my black bra and matching thong. Wrapping his fingers inside my thong again, he looked down at me, appreciating my curves and making me feel sexy with just a glance of that dark gaze. His other hand traveled down until he found the clasp of my bra. With a snap of his fingers, he got it open...and let it drop to the floor.

I wanted to stare at his perfect body as he stood in his boxers, but I was too entranced by the expression on his face. He looked at me like he'd never wanted a woman more, like he didn't know what part of my body he liked the most. He stared at my tits like he'd never seen a woman naked before. His large palm cupped the left one, and he gave it a manly squeeze before his eyes lifted to meet mine. "Damn." That was all he said—and that was all he needed to say.

His thumb swiped over my nipple as he lowered his mouth to my neck. His warm lips collided with my skin, and he started to kiss me everywhere, his warm breath falling across my skin like the Tuscan breeze. With one hand on my tit while the other still squeezed my ass, he enjoyed me like a starving man in the buffet line.

I closed my eyes and rolled my head back, letting him devour me. My pussy ached because I wanted him so much, wanted a big dick inside me to make me feel like a woman. It was an out-of-body experience because I didn't feel like myself at all. I felt like the most beautiful woman in the world when he kissed me like that.

The harder he squeezed my curves, the harder I breathed. He gripped me so tightly that I nearly yelped in his ear, but I liked the firmness of his grasp, the way he treated me like I could handle the pressure.

His hand pushed my thong over my ass, and his fingers slid down to my entrance. His arm was long enough that he could easily slide two fingers inside me, curving all the way around my ass to reach.

I sucked a breath between my teeth when I felt him penetrate me, my eyes closing as I felt him slide into my slickness. Now I could feel how wet I was, feel the moisture as it stuck between my thighs.

He kept his lips near my ear. "Damn, again." He slowly fingered me as he turned to look me in the eye, to watch my reaction to his large fingers inside my small slit. He wore the same expression that he'd had with the blond woman, a look that said he was really enjoying this.

My fingers pushed his boxers down, getting them over his hips until his cock came free. With a thick crown that looked fit for a king and a shaft that rivaled a baseball bat, his dick was probably the source of his arrogance... and I couldn't blame him for it. He had a man's dick, impressively thick and beautifully long. The vein along the shaft was pulsing, leading right up to the crown. I stared at it the way he stared at me. "Damn..." He was bigger than any other man I'd been with, thicker than any other man I'd been with. He'd make me a fully new woman because he would stretch me out to wider capacity.

He stepped out of his clothes and shoes, glorious in his nakedness. He had the perfect physique, strong, tall, and powerful. With tanned skin and tight muscles, he was the kind of man who could bring home a different woman every night...which he did. The only imperfection was a scar on his left shoulder, a discoloration that showed it was an old injury, not a birthmark.

I imagined taking him on my back, the best way for me to come with a man. But with a dick like that, it probably didn't matter what position we were in. I moved to the bed and got on all fours, my back arched as deep as I could so my ass would be high in the air. I kept my head up and looked at him over my shoulder.

He stared at my ass with his hand around his dick. He slowly jerked himself as he gazed at my dripping pussy. He'd managed to transfer my slickness from his fingers to his length, giving himself lube to jerk off easily.

I studied the way his wrist moved as he jerked himself from mid-base to his balls. He couldn't even get his entire dick with the motion because he was too big. I didn't know how that dick was going to fit inside me, but once it was there, I would never want it to leave.

He fished a condom out of his jeans. Slowly, he rolled down the latex until it hit his balls, securing it in place so he could fuck me hard without slipping. He left a large pouch at the front—like he intended to give me a big load.

When he finally let his knees sink into the mattress, I felt the dip of the bed as my stomach tightened. I'd never been so eager to be fucked by a man, to have a dick sink all the way inside until he tapped against my cervix.

He positioned himself right up against my ass then directed his tip to my entrance.

I could feel the push, feel the enormous crown struggle to sink inside my tight little cunt. I'd been with many men, so I was no virgin, but I could barely get him to fit. It didn't matter how aroused I was, it wasn't enough to get him to slide inside with no resistance.

Maverick gripped my shoulder and kept me still as he pushed himself inside. The crown finally stretched me apart so he could make his entrance, slowly sliding through my moisture so the rest of the shaft could follow.

Jesus Christ. I closed my eyes because it hurt...it hurt so

fucking good. My pussy couldn't take another centimeter. His size was my breaking point, and I felt like I was losing my virginity all over again.

He kept sinking until his balls hit my ass. "Fuck..." His fingers dug into my shoulder while his other hand slapped my ass.

I panted because it felt so good. We'd barely even started, and I wanted to come around his dick already. I wanted to get on my knees and bow to this man for being god's gift to women.

He pulled my shoulder back so I was arched, relying on him to keep me held up at this angle.

He was buried deep inside me, both arms holding my body against his chest. He gave me a few gentle pumps, getting used to the tightness, before he started to pound into me.

I held on to his arms for balance and bounced back into him, moaning right from the beginning. My pussy fucked his dick as hard as his dick fucked me. Our bodies smacked together because we were both working so hard, slamming into each other so we could enjoy the high our bodies produced.

My head tilted back, and I moaned like a whore who was paid to scream. "God...yes."

His hands tightened on my arms, and he slammed that big dick inside me. "You like that?"

"Yes...yes." It felt so good, I wanted to cry. It hit the sweet spot, satisfied my cravings. All this time, I'd been having sex with boys, when I should have been having sex with men. This was a dick worth coming around. This was a dick to beg for. "Don't stop...please." My hands moved to my cheeks, and I pulled them apart, just so he could fuck me even deeper.

His hips worked a little harder, and like a machine, he fucked me nonstop, his endurance deserving of a medal. He worked his body hard to please me, to tear my pussy apart with his girth.

It hurt the entire time, but I loved the pain. I loved the way it made me feel...like I'd never really been fucked in my entire life. I bit my bottom lip and moaned, tears in my eyes because of both the pain and the pleasure. Instead of taking minutes to come, it only took a couple of seconds. I kept my cheeks apart and closed my eyes as the flash of heat traveled through me, burning the tips of my fingers and toes. A veil of desire spread across my vision, making everything blurry because I couldn't focus on seeing...only on feeling. I didn't care that I hated this man, that I didn't want him to have a bigger ego than he already did. I came around his dick and whimpered his name. "Maverick..." My hips started to buck automatically as tears glistened in my eyes. I'd always been a moaner when I had an orgasm, but never a crier. But now I cried for this man...because it was so damn good.

A moan escaped from his throat, like he could feel how tight I was getting around his length. He increased his pace just a little more, to give me all of himself as he finished. He lasted long enough to let me finish, to enjoy every second of the orgasm until it started to fade like smoke to the ceiling.

Then he came. With a masculine grunt, he shoved his length deep inside me and shuddered as he released, his come exploding into the space in the condom. His hands tightened on my arms, and he moaned again.

I kept my cheeks apart, knowing he was probably staring at my asshole as he finished.

After making me come like that, he could stare at whatever he wanted.

He finished then pulled out, making my pussy feel several inches wider than when he first entered me. He released my arms a second later, letting my body fall forward because I hadn't been expecting it.

I let my body drop to the mattress because I was tired and satisfied. My pussy throbbed because of his size and destruction, but it also throbbed because it felt so damn good. I'd never been fucked like that. I'd never come like that.

Maverick disposed of the condom in the bathroom then pulled on his clothes. He didn't say a word to me or even look at me. Like I was just a stranger he would never see again, he flattened his shirt against his stomach then walked out.

I didn't know what I was expecting him to do. Sex wouldn't change his behavior. He would still be the indifferent asshole he'd always been. He would barge into my room without knocking and then leave it just as abruptly. I wasn't a date, so there was no reason for us to sleep in each other's beds.

Even though it wasn't even eight yet, I dug under the covers and closed my eyes...falling asleep just minutes later.

19

MAVERICK

MY MOTORBIKE WAS ON THE GROUND, HIDDEN IN THE HIGH blades of grass. With a bulletproof helmet on my head and the communication device clipped to my ear, I could hear what the men were saying over the intercom—including my father.

"They're two miles away." My father gave orders to the rest of the men, falling into the role of dictator so well. His voice was level and calm, even though his entire purpose was riding on this event.

"Got it." I sat in the countryside with the stars as company. There were other men hidden along the route, but since they were invisible, it was easy to forget they were there. On this summer night, the stars were bright overhead, brilliant because Florence was an hour into the distance. A slight breeze moved across my neck, giving me a respite from the helmet and leather jacket.

My thoughts drifted to Arwen, but when they became sexual, I tuned her out of my mind. I couldn't afford to be distracted by the good fuck I'd had a couple of hours ago. Who knew sex with your wife could be so fun?

A minute later, the Hummers sped down the road. Ramon was meeting with one of his clients for a drug deal. Little did he know they would never make it. Once the headlights were gone and they were several feet in front of us, I kicked the bike to life and started to follow them. "I'm on his tail."

"Alright. We'll begin the assault now. Sneak up behind them—don't let them see you."

I kept trailing the Hummers, staying a good distance away so they wouldn't see me in their rearview mirrors. I saw the lights of my dad's team up ahead. The Hummer crossed the road and blocked their path.

That when the shots began to fire.

The intercom was silent.

I accelerated down the road, the bike quiet compared to all the commotion up ahead. I was only a few feet away when something took a turn for the worse.

Yells sounded through the intercom.

Now my father wasn't so calm. "I need backup."

Ramon was my first priority, but not when my father's life was at risk. I didn't need to think twice about it before I reacted, changing my goal instantly. "I'm on my way."

"No." He yelled into the intercom. "Get Ramon. He's all that—" He screamed over the line.

My wrist cranked the gas, and I sped past the three Hummers. Gunshots were firing off everywhere, sparks of light in the darkness. My eyes scanned the blackness as I searched for my father, frantically trying to find him.

I skidded to a halt across the pavement when I saw my

father fighting off two men. Every time a gun was pointed at his face, he managed to slam it down before he took a bullet to the head. He'd obviously been disarmed. Otherwise, he would have shot the assholes right then.

I jumped off the bike and sprinted toward the commotion, pulling out my pistol when I got close. I shot the first guy and forced him to the ground, but another had his gun aimed at my father. My father was too busy staring at me in horror to notice.

"Move!" I sprinted toward the gun, aiming my gun so I could take him out before he could pull the trigger. But even if my shot was enough to stop him, his finger would squeeze the trigger automatically. I only had one option.

I fired my weapon then slammed into my father, pushing him to the ground.

Then the pain shot up my arm, the nerves firing off in protest. I'd been shot before, and the shock was the worst part. The body immediately went into survival mode, dulling the senses to keep the systems calm.

I slammed into the pavement and gripped my arm, feeling the blood soak my jacket.

My bullet hit the man in the neck, but he was still alive.

My father picked up my dropped gun and finished him off. When he turned to look at me, I expected to see fatherly terror in his eyes. I expected him to rip off my jacket, apply pressure, and finally give me respect for what I had done.

But it wasn't forthcoming.

"I told you to get Ramon."

I gripped my arm to stop the bleeding. "You're kidding me, right?"

"No." He walked over to me and pressed his foot against my wound. "When I tell you to do something, you do it."

I groaned as the blood poured out. "Jesus!"

He pulled his foot off and continued to stare at me with disappointment. The gunfight started to die down as the tables turned. Our men seemed to have gained the upper hand, and Ramon's men didn't have a chance. If Ramon fled, he wouldn't get far.

"I saved your life, asshole."

With that icy-cold countenance, he looked at me like I was dirt on the bottom of his shoe. "My life means nothing without Ramon. You better hope he didn't get away. Otherwise, I'll step on your arm until I break it."

AT SIX IN THE MORNING, we returned to my estate and drove to the barn that was out of sight from all the roads. To any onlooker, it seemed like an ordinary barn, something the cows used to get out of the rain. Little did they know, it would double as a prison.

I didn't make a complaint about my arm. I wrapped gauze around it and applied pressure to stop the bleeding, but now that the adrenaline had passed, all I was left with was the pain. I rode in the front seat with my father, Ramon knocked out in the rear.

This was a fucking nightmare.

We parked the Hummer then proceeded to drag Ramon's unconscious body into the barn. I helped even though a bullet was still lodged in my flesh.

My father didn't bat an eye over it, didn't even care.

We dragged Ramon into the cell designed to hold his body. It had a bucket of fresh water, a bucket for shitting, and hay on the ground for sleeping. We dropped him in the center of the concrete stable, watching the bastard lie there unconscious. He had one window at the very top, but it was too small for anyone to climb through.

My father spat on him before he shut the door and locked it.

I studied my father as he secured the padlock, wondering if he was feeling victorious now that his enemy had been captured.

But he seemed like the same bitter man as before.

"What now?" My workers would steer clear of his cell. One of my men would make sure he had food and water every day, plus a fresh bucket to shit in every day. But it would be pointless to keep him for long when he was of no use alive.

"Nothing." He walked away from the door and headed back to the car.

"You aren't going to torture him right away?" I caught up with my father, my heart beating so hard because of the pain in my arm. I broke out in an intense sweat because it was getting more difficult to keep going when I was getting weaker by the second.

"No." We got into the car. "I'll let you know when I'm ready."

After all this work, he was just going to let him sit in a cell? I'd assumed my father would start to torture him immediately, even if he was unconscious.

My father turned down the dirt road and approached my estate, ready to drop me off. When he pulled up to the house, he hit the brakes instead of turning off the car. He clearly expected me to jump out and walk inside without another word.

How did my father turn into this? "I'm fine, by the way."

He stared straight ahead, ignoring my sarcasm. "You've been shot before. You'll be shot again someday. It'll be fine."

"You aren't the least bit concerned?" I cocked an eyebrow. "I could have died."

He sighed in annoyance. "But you didn't. Now go inside. It's been a long night."

I lingered in the car, so angry, I didn't know what to do. If my father was going to be this cold, I shouldn't have bothered helping him in the first place. I married a stranger to get this information, but he brushed off my sacrifice. I took a bullet for him, but he didn't give a damn. There was nothing I could do right—only wrong. "I turned thirty a couple of weeks ago..." Birthdays were an arbitrary celebration. I didn't even like birthdays. But it stung the most that he'd forgotten it. Mom used to force us to gather around a birthday cake and exchange presents. Making me have a memorable evening with our family was her gift to me—a gift of love. Now that the glue that held the four of us together was gone, we were just three strangers.

My father still didn't look at me. "You want me to give you a present or something?"

The sarcasm in his voice made me wish I hadn't taken that bullet for him. If I'd just done as he asked, he might be dead right now. I would have mourned his passing since this sad conversation never would have taken place. We finally completed the job we set out to do—to give my mother justice. But he was still the cold bastard I despised. I grabbed the handle and opened the door. "I wish I'd let you take that bullet...and I wished it had killed you."

I SAT at the counter in the kitchen with my arm extended. Abigail pulled back the gauze and revealed the damage. She had her suture kit ready to go, but she still looked disappointed when she saw the wound that destroyed my flesh. "Mr. DeVille...what happened?"

I grabbed the vodka on the counter and took a drink. "I was shot—obviously."

She was my servant, but she didn't hesitate to give me an attitude. She glared at me before she took the warm towel and wiped away the dried blood that stuck to the skin of my shoulder. "Don't be a smartass." When all the blood was wiped away, she grabbed her tweezers and gently slipped the tips inside my flesh to fetch the bullet.

I took another drink even though I didn't care for vodka.

The sound of quick footsteps ended in the kitchen, and Arwen's gasp entered my ears a moment later. "Oh shit..." She came to my side and watched Abigail pull the bullet out of my flesh and drop it onto the plate sitting on the counter. Arwen's hands gripped my healthy arm, and she looked terrified by the scene that unfolded in front of her. "Are you alright?"

"If I were going to die, it would have happened hours ago." I watched Abigail open her suture kit and begin to close the wound.

"Maverick." She kept staring at me, her hand gripping my arm. "What happened?"

"Is that not obvious?" I asked, still being a smartass.

"If you weren't being sutured right now, I'd slap you." She was in a black nightdress, a halter top that was so thin, it showed her hard nipples through the fabric. It was difficult to believe we'd been fucking just twelve hours ago. Now a bullet had just been pulled out of me.

"I'd help you." Abigail kept her eyes on her hands, closing up the wound with the thread.

"Should you go to a hospital?" Arwen asked.

"No." I never went to the hospital. I'd have to be on my death bed to resort to that.

"And you don't think you should?" Arwen asked incredulously.

"No. I've been shot before—not a big deal." My father certainly thought it was nothing to worry about.

Abigail finished her task then closed everything up. "I'll get you some antibiotics tomorrow just to make sure you don't get an infection."

"Thanks, Abigail." I rolled down my shirt sleeve and hopped off the stool.

Arwen followed me. "Are you sure you're okay? Who gets shot and brushes it off like that?"

"Men." I headed up the stairs.

She stuck to my side. "What happened tonight? Is your father okay?"

I wished he weren't okay. "We got Ramon. He's in the barn."

"Here?" she asked in surprise. "Why?"

Because that's what my father wanted...and he always got what he wanted. "It's convenient."

"So you're going to torture him a couple of acres away?"

She followed me all the way up the stairs and to the hallway that led to my room.

"Yep." I reached my bedroom and walked inside, eager to take a shower to wash off all the grass and dried blood. "I'm not in the mood for chitchat. Get out so I can go to sleep."

"How can I leave you alone when you've just been shot?"

Instead of being touched by her concern, I was just annoyed. "There's nothing you can do for me. Now, let me go to sleep." I started to strip off my clothes without waiting for her to leave. She'd already seen me naked, so it didn't matter.

She stood by the door, still watching me with that concerned gaze.

"Don't make me ask you again." I didn't want to be an ass when her only crime was compassion, but I was seriously not in the mood tonight. "I've been up for almost thirty-six hours. We aren't doing this now."

"You'll say the same thing in the morning."

Yeah, I probably would.

"I know there's something bothering you, something you're keeping from me." With her arms crossed over her chest, she watched me like she was reading words that appeared on my forehead.

My father couldn't care less if I died...that was the secret I was keeping from the whole world. "It's none of your business, Arwen. Now, get the fuck out—before I make you."

ARWEN

WHEN I CAME DOWN FOR BREAKFAST THE NEXT DAY, MAVERICK was nowhere to be seen. "Did he already leave for work?"

"No." Abigail stood at the sink and washed the dishes she'd used to make breakfast. "He's resting in bed today. I told him if he moved, he wouldn't get anything to eat. He made the right call and decided to stay put."

"Good." He shouldn't be running around with a wound like that. "Anything I can do to help?"

"I don't think there's anything anyone can do. Mr. DeVille can be a bastard sometimes…" Abigail was a woman in her midforties, someone who was a faithful servant but also spoke her mind. And her heart seemed to be in the right place. "All we can do is hope he gets the rest he needs. But you know how he is…"

Yes, he was a huge bastard. "Yeah, I do."

I headed to the third floor and walked down the hallway to his bedroom. The door was closed, so I tapped my knuckles against the wood, thinking of the time I'd spied on him when he was fucking someone. It was a huge violation of his privacy, but I couldn't help it...and I didn't regret it. It led to me getting the best night of sex in my life.

His deep voice sounded like a distant drum. "Come in."

I stepped inside and saw him sitting up in bed. Shirtless and in just his sweatpants on top of the sheets, his white gauze was visible around his shoulder. He was scrolling through his phone, probably assuming I was Abigail who'd come to clean.

I shut the door behind me. "You look better today."

When he heard my voice, he looked up from his phone and abandoned whatever he was doing. He was calmer than he was yesterday, and the shadow along his jawline was thicker because he'd skipped the shave that morning. His eyes were the same color as his coffee on the nightstand, dark brown. "Yes?" Like we hadn't had sex just a few days ago, he was cold and hostile.

I sat at the edge of the bed. "Wanted to see if there was something I could do for you."

"No." He looked at his phone again.

This man couldn't accept compliments. He couldn't accept help either. He couldn't accept anything. "I can help at the factory if you need anything. Or if you just want some company, I can help with that too."

"I know you don't know me very well, but I'm not much of a talker."

"Yeah...I picked up on that."

He lowered his phone again. "Then go."

I noticed he had no problem being sympathetic if I was in pain. Whatever it was, he was there for me. Not once did he make fun of me. He always turned into the crutch that supported my grief. But for whatever reason, he wouldn't let me do the same for him. He kept everything bottled up inside, refusing to acknowledge whatever was bothering him. "You don't trust anyone, do you?"

His eyes slowly turned to me, narrowing slightly like those words hit a sensitive nerve. "No. But you don't trust anyone either."

"That's not true...I trust you."

He set his phone on the bed beside him, still looking strong despite the injury he suffered. His chest was still as strong as ever, powerful muscles constantly throbbing under his tight skin. "You shouldn't."

"Why not? You promised you would never hurt me, and you kept that promise. You're there for me in my darkest times. You've never put me down when I already felt terrible. You always pick me up. I trust you more than I trust anyone else in this world."

"You said you didn't like me."

"I don't always have to like you to trust you. You can be an asshole sometimes, but that doesn't mean you're a liar. You're there when it matters, and that's what counts."

He shifted his gaze away.

"You told me we were allies. If you're my ally, that means I'm yours."

He turned back to look at me. "What's your point?"

"That you can trust me. I know you well enough to see when something is weighing you down, when you have a boulder on each shoulder. I know you well enough to see the irritation in your eyes...and know it has nothing to do with me. You obviously don't have anyone to talk to, but you can talk to me." I stared at him and hoped he would open up to me, tell me what happened last night.

But he was still cold.

"Maverick..."

"Why do you want me to talk to you so badly?"

"Because I care about you. I was happy when you returned, but devastated when I saw you'd been shot. I'm glad you're okay... I mean that." The only time he flinched was when something heartfelt came from my mouth. His eyes blinked and he tensed slightly, like my words hurt him rather than helped him. When I knew he wouldn't respond in any way, I finally gave up. I didn't understand this man, and if he never let me in, I would never understand him. I turned away and looked at his bedroom wall.

Silence stretched for a long time, as if Maverick didn't have a single thing to say to me. He was closed like a steel gate. Nothing could get through—not even a key. Eventually, his deep voice broke through the silence. "My father is the reason I got shot."

My eyes stayed on the wall, but my heart started to clench in pain and rage. I slowly turned back to him, flabbergasted by what I'd just heard.

He leaned his head against the headboard and looked away, like eye contact was too much for him. "I was supposed to go after Ramon, but I could tell my father was in trouble by listening to the comms. I went after my father instead...didn't think twice about it. When I got there, I shot one of the men. But another was about to take out my father. I pushed him out of the way and took the bullet myself..."

He risked his life to save his father...even though that man was an asshole. If that wasn't loyalty, I didn't know what was.

"Instead of being pleased, he was disappointed. He stepped on my arm and made it bleed more. He said Ramon was the only thing that mattered...and I was stupid for disobeying him."

"You saved his life, and that was his response?"

A wounded expression came over his face, looking lost. "Yes."

I hadn't liked his father the second I met him, but I hadn't thought he was capable of something so malicious.

"And he's shot me before...when he didn't get his way."

My eyes widened.

His hand moved to his injury. "Same spot, actually. At least the scars will be in one place..."

"Jackass."

He made a slight shrug. "As stupid and insignificant as this sounds, he didn't remember my birthday. It really bothered me for some reason, made me realize how much my mother held the four of us together."

What kind of father was he? "The four of you?" I'd never asked if he had a sibling. If he did, I didn't notice them at the wedding.

"I have a younger sister."

"Oh...did I meet her at the wedding?" There were a lot of people around that day.

He shook his head. "She wasn't there."

What kind of family was this?

"I know your father did a stupid thing, but even when your mother was gone, he still loved you. I respected him for that. Everything I said at the funeral...I meant it." He finally turned his head back and looked at me, finding the strength to meet my gaze when there was pain in his eyes. "When my father dropped me off yesterday, I said I wished he were dead... He didn't seem to care."

Maverick's story made me miss my father more. He was always affectionate and kind to me, never downplaying his love even in front of his friends. "I don't understand how your father can be that way. There's no excuse. Why do you still talk to him?"

"Our lives are too intertwined. We used to work together, the cheese company is technically his because he's still family, and I guess I thought things might change when we got Ramon. Might give him closure. It's hard to believe, but when my mother was still here, he was a good guy. He was affectionate, he did remember my birthday. But after what happened to her...all of his compassion disappeared. He turned into a whole different person."

When my mother died, my father was different too. But he never stopped loving me as a result. "That's no excuse..."

"No, it's not. But I guess I still hope that he'll come back...someday."

That was never going to happen. But I kept my opinion to myself.

"There. I told you everything. Now what?" He turned cold again, like he resented me for opening up.

"Now, I can share your pain. Now, I can understand you. Now, I can make you feel less alone." My hand moved to his, and I interlocked our fingers, just the way I had at the funeral. I stared at our joined hands and felt the pain in my heart. He didn't deserve this. No son deserved to be treated so poorly by his father. "Thank you for telling me..."

"You weren't going to leave me alone until I did."

"But still..." I lifted my gaze and met his.

He watched me for a long time, his brown eyes a little less hostile. He didn't pull his hand away and let our fingers rest together. Even when he was in pain, he still wore the most handsome expression, his jawline so tight, he seemed to be brooding all the time. But the look was sexy on him.

"I noticed you have a TV in here." It hung on the wall above the fireplace, directly facing his bed.

He watched me, unsure why I'd said that.

"Since you don't have anything to do today, how about we watch movies together? We can watch a couple of your favorites, and I can watch a couple of mine."

"I don't watch TV."

"Then why do you have it?" I countered.

He smiled slightly, like he knew he'd bested me. "Honestly? When I watch porn, I watch it on TV. Easier than using a laptop."

It was a dirty thing to say, but I admired him for being honest. It was one of the things I liked about him, the fact that he didn't care about my opinion. If I thought he was an asshole, he would still act like an asshole. "I didn't think you watched porn."

He cocked an eyebrow, like I'd just said something crazy. "If a guy tells you he doesn't watch porn, he's full of shit. Just so you know."

"That's not what I meant. It just seems like you get the real thing a lot..."

The corner of his mouth rose in a smile. "Sometimes it takes too much work. You just want to get off and be done with it. No talking. No drinking. No sleepovers."

"Well...how about we find something to watch?"

"You want to watch porn in here?" he asked, lightening up a little more.

"No." I smacked his hand playfully. "I meant, let's find a movie to watch—one that isn't X-rated."

"You don't like porn? You should give it a try."

"I do like porn," I said honestly. "I just don't watch it on my TV. And I probably don't watch it as much as you do."

He nearly did a double take at my response. "You don't seem like a woman who would be into that."

"I told you I was good in bed. I didn't just get my moves from experience…"

Now he looked at me with new eyes. "Maybe you're right…maybe we can be friends."

I rolled my eyes and rose to my feet. "I'm going to change. I'll be back in a bit."

"You could just take one of my shirts. It's not like I haven't seen you naked."

I opened one of his drawers and pulled out a shirt, something that fit him snugly but would be a blanket on me. "Alright." I moved to the bathroom.

"You can't change out here?"

"Nope. You don't just get to see this whenever you feel like it."

"You are my wife…"

I smiled before I shut the door. "And that means I run the show."

21

MAVERICK

MY DAY WAS SPENT IN BED—WATCHING MOVIES.

I hadn't done that since I was a kid.

And I'd never had a woman in my bed without fucking. Arwen lay next to me under the sheets, eating the popcorn Abigail brought up an hour ago. She stayed on her side of the bed and didn't try to cuddle with me.

Good. Because I would have pushed her off.

When the movie ended, she propped her head on her hand and looked at me. "What did you think?"

"Porn would have been better."

She rolled her eyes but chuckled at the same time.

I was surprised I'd told her so much about my life. I never told anyone anything, not my friends or my sister. The idea of sharing those intimate thoughts and feelings made me feel weak. Actually saying them out loud made me feel like a pussy.

But it also made me feel better.

I didn't know what this woman was to me anymore. On

the outside, she was just my wife. But in reality, she was my friend...and someone I was attracted to.

How could I not be? Even with messy hair and a baggy shirt, she was still stunning. There was a kernel stuck in her teeth earlier, but I somehow found it cute rather than grotesque. I ended up spending the entire day with her, doing absolutely nothing.

I wasn't the kind of man that did nothing. The only reason why I did today was because my injury forced me to. But spending it with her made it seem a little less unbearable.

She set the empty bowl on the nightstand then looked at the time on my alarm clock. "Wow...time flies when you're having fun."

I followed her gaze and realized she was right. We'd spent the entire day in bed, eating and watching whatever she picked out. I wasn't bored like I'd thought I would be.

She adjusted her pillow then lay down again, her hair falling perfectly over the soft cotton. The sheets were around her waist, and my t-shirt didn't fit her curves well because it was many sizes too big. But she happened to lie in the perfect position, at the perfect angle, and she looked beautiful.

Her thick eyelashes cast a light shadow over her blue eyes. Sometimes her mascara would smear on my pillow-cases, but I didn't mind in the least. She was the first woman to wear one of my t-shirts to bed, and it looked better on her than it ever did on me.

Now I ignored the TV and watched her instead. My mind drifted back to the evening when she'd begged me to fuck her. All of her restraint disappeared, and she finally gave in to the throbbing desire between her legs. My cock sank inside her, finding a home inside that wet slit. She had the sexiest ass, so I was happy to fuck her that way, like she was a bitch in heat. I stared at her asshole as I came, in love with the lovely curves of her body.

The pain in my shoulder dulled when the arousal took over. Now I wanted to take her on her back, to stare at those sexy tits as I fucked her hard into the mattress. I wanted to see her expression when she came. Listening to her moan was just as beautiful as when she sang, but I wanted to see it with my own eyes, see those plump lips part as she screamed.

She kept watching the TV, oblivious to my intentions.

My cock hardened in my sweatpants the longer I stared at her. Ever since our night together, we hadn't discussed what happened. It seemed to be a memory neither one of us mentioned. I wasn't sure what would happen when we were finished. I enjoyed fucking her, so I assumed I would want to fuck her again.

I definitely wanted to fuck her again.

I wanted a casual relationship where we didn't talk about it all the time. It seemed like she could handle it. After all, she was the one who assumed I would become obsessed with her...which was ridiculous.

So I went for it.

I rolled toward her then dug my hand into her hair, capturing her attention as I lowered my head. My lips found hers, tasting like butter from the popcorn. My free hand snaked up her thigh until my fingers felt the soft material of her panties. Once my mouth was on hers, I felt the electricity burn my spine from top to bottom. It even hit my dick, making it twitch with a jolt. My shoulder screamed in agony, but that wasn't enough to stop me.

Her lips were hesitant at first because she hadn't been

expecting my kiss. But once she felt it, her hand went to my bare chest, and she dug her long nails into me. After a few breaths, she kissed me harder, giving me her tongue right from the beginning.

She was a damn good kisser.

We fell into a rhythm naturally, taking and giving in perfect succession. I knew how to suck her bottom lip to make her nails dig into me a little harder, and she did a sexy swipe with her tongue that was so amazing, my dick nearly broke through my sweatpants. I could feel the hardness of her ring whenever she touched me, the piece of jewelry that bonded her to me in the eyes of the world.

I gripped the back of her panties and slowly started to pull them down, but I stilled when I felt the pain in my shoulder. A hot explosion of agony ran through the nerves and made me still.

Arwen stopped kissing me when she felt me tense up. The arousal slowly died away in her gaze, replaced by concern. It was the same way she looked at me when she realized I'd been shot. It was like she really cared...which was more than most people could say.

My lips returned to hers because I wanted to keep going. I refused to give in to weakness, to let my pain hold me back. I'd been shot before, and I kept up my daily routine, not letting my injury become a handicap. Even if it hurt more this time around, I wouldn't let it slow me down.

She gripped my healthy arm and forced me to roll to my back. "Maverick, you're injured."

"I'm fine." I moved up again.

She pushed me back down, finding a burst of strength that belied her small stature. "No."

"No one tells me no."

"Well, that's about to change." She kept one hand planted on my chest then straddled my hips, sitting right on my hard dick and keeping me still. "The more you push yourself, the longer it'll take to heal."

"You think I care?"

"You should. And why hurt yourself doing something I could do?" She grabbed her shirt and slowly peeled it over her head, revealing her perfect body in a black bra. She tossed the shirt aside then reached behind her back to unclasp it.

Once her tits were on display, I shut my mouth. Perky and round, they were the nicest pair of tits I'd ever seen. Lovely flesh with small nipples, they were perfect for tit-fucking. They were also perfect for staring at. My cock twitched against her bottom.

She ran her fingers through her hair then flipped it over one shoulder, regarding me with a cool and confident gaze. Now she sat in just her panties, a cute pink thong that looked so beautiful against her pale skin.

My fingers found their way into the material, getting wrapped up in the lace as my breathing increased. My cock could already imagine how tight her pussy was, how good it felt to be inside her. He twitched harder against her, excited for the panties to disappear so he could slide right in.

She grabbed the top of my sweatpants and boxers and pulled them down, letting my eager cock come free, already drooling at the tip. She moved my bottoms until my balls were free of the fabric before she climbed back up my body and held herself on top of me, her long brown hair dragging across my skin.

My hands immediately went to her tits, my thumbs brushing across her pebbling nipples. I squeezed the firm flesh and looked into her eyes, no longer frustrated that I wasn't the one on top.

She leaned down and kissed me, giving me her tongue right away.

I moaned into her mouth and squeezed her tits, slipping away into the cloud of sex.

She kissed me with the same sexiness as before, taking her time when she felt my lips. When her tongue swiped across mine, it was the sexiest thing ever. Even when she took all the control, she somehow made it sexy. I was always in charge—but I didn't mind handing over the reins.

She suddenly broke away, leaving my lips in agony as she turned around. With her ass in my face, she leaned down and dragged her tongue along my dick, starting with the tip and moving to the base.

Holy fucking shit.

She pointed my cock in the air then shoved it into her mouth, sliding down as my dick moved deeper and deeper down her throat.

And her beautiful ass was in my face.

Fuck, I could come right then.

My hands squeezed her cheeks as I felt her warm mouth take me over and over. I breathed hard, barely able to keep my eyes open because I was slipping away so fast. My cock wanted to fire a cannonball of come deep into her throat.

I peeled her thong down and stared right at her asshole, the sexy little hole that tormented me. Farther I tugged until her pussy was revealed, shining with the arousal that lined her perfect lips.

If she kept this up, I would come before I even got the chance to please her.

She shoved my dick far into her mouth, so far that she nearly gagged. Then she turned back around, pushing her underwear off her hips so she was completely naked.

My arms automatically pushed me up so I leaned against the headboard, my fat dick soaked in her saliva. My eyes were a little unfocused because I was so hard up, I could barely control myself. The image of her ass in my face would stay with me forever—and even replace my porn videos for a while.

She helped herself to my nightstand and fished out the stack of condoms sitting there. My wedding ring sat at the bottom, untouched since the day I took it off at the end of our reception. With all the confidence in the world, she ripped the foil packet while holding my gaze, like the burning ache in her legs wasn't enough to disrupt her composure. She lowered the latex onto my dick, and like she'd done it a million times, rolled it to the base.

I'd never wanted a woman more in my life.

She straddled my hips once again, and with her hand to guide her, slowly lowered herself onto my length, sinking down until she had every inch lodged deep inside her. Her nipples turned hard, her breathing became uneven, and she rolled her head back like she hadn't been expecting such a fat dick.

My hands went to her hips, and I squeezed her hard, my fingers digging into the softest flesh I'd ever felt. My cock throbbed inside her, making itself at home in her perfect pussy. I inhaled a deep breath and felt my lungs stretch as all my nerves fired off in pleasure. The pain in my shoulder was forgotten.

Her arms wrapped around my neck, and she pressed her face close to mine, her breathing filling the silence between us. The TV faded into background noise that neither one of us noticed. Her pretty eyes were locked on me, her pussy expanding to take every single inch of my dick—length and width.

My fingers kneaded her perfect ass, squeezing the muscle and pulling it apart as I imagined that sexy asshole just sitting there. I was buried to the hilt inside her and so happy, forgetting all the bullshit that happened the night before.

I was fucking my wife—and loving every second of it.

She started to move up and down, arching her back at the same time to really feel the grooves of my dick. She watched my expression like she was turned by my arousal the way I was turned on by hers. With our eyes locked together, we got off on each other, writhing and panting in ecstasy.

Damn, she knew how to ride a dick.

I gripped her ass and assisted her in her movements, picking up the pace because I wanted to fuck her so hard. I wanted to pound that pussy like it'd never been pounded before. But I was the one sitting on my ass, so I had to make her do it.

She rose to the challenge.

She moaned in my face, the noises she made so innately sexy. She hit the most beautiful notes, like keys on a piano. I recognized the melodic voice she used in the theatre, the way she projected herself to an auditorium full of people. As a result, her moans sounded like an erotic song.

Sexiest thing I'd ever heard.

I spanked her ass as she rode me, loving that perky ass on my dick. I wanted to fuck her through the night, fuck her until she came over and over. My dick wanted to live inside this pussy forever, to visit her warm mouth and tight asshole from time to time. I protected this woman far more than she realized, and I thought I deserved hot sex in exchange. She had to work for my protection, work if she wanted to be a naïve sheep living in a meadow with no worries. As the wolf, I never let my guard down. I peered into the night and saw monsters while others assumed they were shadows. I anticipated the worst and hoped for the best. I never slept, not unless I knew my sheep were safe.

Not unless I knew my wife was safe.

IT TOOK days for me to recover. Maybe it was a slower process than last time because I'd already been shot in the same area before. The nerves and tissue were permanently damaged beyond repair, and now I just added more fuel to the fire.

Arwen spent time in my room and kept me company.

We screwed a lot.

She climbed on my lap and fucked me over and over.

I didn't mind in the least.

Every night, she excused herself and went to sleep in her own room.

I was finally on my feet again, the wound closed up without sign of infection. It still hurt a bit, but unless I started to move it again normally, it would take much longer to heal. I showered and got ready for the day, skipping my usual workout because my body wasn't ready for that just yet.

When I came downstairs, Arwen was already there. She looked at her phone while she munched on toast, eggs, and sautéed veggies. Her coffee was steaming hot. She looked up when she saw me sit across from her. "You look good."

I could never take a compliment, not even now. I ignored what she said and poured myself a cup of coffee.

Arwen ignored my silence and sipped from her mug. "Are you going back to work today?"

"Yes."

"Take it easy. Don't overdo it."

"Don't worry about me, alright?" Just because we were fucking pretty often didn't mean I owed her anything. As far as I was concerned, we were still two people living under the same roof—and nothing more.

"If you weren't sneaking off into the night and getting shot, I wouldn't have to worry."

I grabbed a piece of toast and smeared it with butter. "I don't need you to worry about me, so don't bother."

She cocked her eyebrow slightly. "If I don't worry about you, who will?"

It was a cold thing to say, but I probably deserved to hear it. She was the one who consoled me on my darkest days, comforted me even when I refused to wear my pain on my sleeve. "Just because we're sleeping together doesn't mean anything has changed."

"I never said anything had changed."

"But you're acting like I owe you something."

She shook her head slightly. "You do owe me something —your friendship. You're the one who told me we were allies. You can stop pushing me away every time we get closer. Trust me, I'm not looking for anything more than sex from you. So you can cut the shit and chill out."

This woman wasn't like the others. "I just want to keep it that way."

"As do I. But I would like for us to be friends and to stop being dicks to each other. Why can't we have that?"

I guess I was too scared to get close to anyone. My mother was gone, my father hated me, and my sister went off the deep end. I'd lost everyone who mattered to me—and it sucked. They say it's better to have loved and lost than not to have loved at all... but that was bullshit. "I just don't want anything more."

"What makes you think I would ever want more from you?" Her eyebrow was still raised. "I think you're a good guy, Maverick. I'm obviously attracted to you. But I'm not looking to make this marriage into a real relationship. You and I are so different that it would never work anyway. But I don't see why we can't have some sense of trust and friendship. I expect you to bring home women, and I'll hook up with men. Sometimes we'll hook up with each other, but that's it. All I want from you is some kind of closeness...because I'm really lonely."

I kept my smartass comments to myself when she revealed something so vulnerable. She'd never said that to me before, admitted she wasn't the strong woman she projected herself to be.

She shrugged. "I've always wanted to fall in love and get married...but now I can't. Logic would argue that I should try to fall in love with you, but that spark just isn't there. They say people fall in love within the first forty-eight hours of meeting someone. If it hasn't happened by now, then we clearly aren't right for each other. But if we really are going to be husband and wife for the rest of our lives, there should be a solid foundation between us. We should be able to trust each other, especially when neither one of us has anyone else."

It was easy to believe her because she seemed so genuine. I never got the impression that her concern for me stemmed from something romantic. Maybe she really did just care about me in a friendly sort of way. "Alright. Then we'll be two people who have casual sex, who are honest with each other, and are friends. But I mean it when I say we'll never be anything more. I will continue to sleep with whoever I want, and I expect you to do the same." I liked my life the way it was. I could give her a partnership and friendship, but that was the extent of my generosity.

"I don't have a problem with that."

I gauged her expression as she said it, and it seemed like she meant it.

"I have one question, though."

I automatically tensed, afraid she would throw a curve ball at me.

"My father said I need to stay married to you forever. But is that really true? Ten years from now, will I really still be in danger? By then, his enemies will have moved on. I'll be forgotten. Is it really necessary for this marriage to be infinite?"

The same thought crossed my mind months ago. I knew she was asking because she was seeking hope. She wanted to know that she might still meet her dream guy and settle down, that this arrangement wasn't forever. "I don't know what's going to happen. When someone dies, the world keeps on turning. People shift their focus to other things."

"That doesn't answer my question."

"I know—because your question can't be answered. I'm not a fortune-teller that can see the future. It's possible the dust will settle and the world will forget your father ever lived. Maybe that will happen in two years, maybe twenty. Or maybe it'll never happen at all. We'll have to be patient and see. In my experience, the world moves on quickly. People adapt, chase the next big thing. And in the underworld, everything changes in a split second. They'll find a bigger fish to catch and forget all about you."

"So, you think our odds are good?"

I shrugged. "I promised your father I would stay married to you forever. So, at the end of the day, it'll be your call."

"So, I could walk away right now if I wanted to?"

"You can walk away whenever you want—but I don't recommend it."

"Does that mean people are after me?" She abandoned her coffee and breakfast, leaning forward over the table as she considered what I'd said.

I drank my coffee and ignored her question.

"Maverick."

I held her gaze but continued to be quiet. "Let me worry about that, alright?"

Her eyes slowly fell when the truth hit her in the face. Her shoulders started to sag, and the fearlessness she always wore was long gone. She wasn't the rambunctious woman with an attitude made of fire. Now she was scared...the fear written on her face. "Why didn't you tell me?"

"Because you're my sheep. You're supposed to keep your head down and graze. I'm the wolf—and I'll chase away the other dogs. That's how this works. That's why you married me."

That didn't chase away her fear. She still looked afraid. "Who is it? What do they want with me?"

To rape her—and then charge money so other men could rape her. "It doesn't matter what they want—they won't get it."

She leaned back in her chair, disconcerted but also touched. Now she understood how instrumental I was to her survival. If I weren't around, she would have been captured long ago. "Thank you…"

She didn't need to thank me. I protected her because I got something out of it. Now I would continue to do so because I was a man of my word. "Don't be scared, Sheep. As long as I'm living, nothing could ever hurt you…I promise."

I was sitting at my desk at the factory when my father called me.

The last time I spoke to him, I told him I wished he were dead.

Knowing him, he would pretend it never happened.

I answered. "Yes?"

"Meet me at the barn." He hung up.

I listened to the line go dead as my suspicion was confirmed. My father cared so little about me that wishing he were dead meant nothing. When I said those words, I meant them, but I also hoped it would spur a conversation, that we would finally discuss the demonic nature of our relationship.

Everything would be out in the open and I could tell him how I felt...but now I realized that was futile.

Nothing would ever change.

My father's soul died the day my mother did. All his love and compassion disappeared too. All that was left was a bitter and hateful old man.

I got into the truck and drove several acres until I reached the barn in the distance, the smell of the cows entering my nose the second I opened the door. The barn was enormous, big enough to house all of my animals during the worst storms.

I walked inside and stopped at the scene before me.

Two women were tied up, their knees against the pile of hay underneath them. Their wrists were bound behind their backs, and their mouths were taped shut. The older one had tears streaming down her cheeks. The younger one looked to be a teenager—and she was in a panic, screaming against the tape that kept her mouth closed.

I lifted my eyes and looked at my father standing over them. "What the fuck is this?" I shut the barn door behind me so no one else could see the criminal activities my father was up to—not that they would say a damn word.

With murder in his eyes, he was unaffected by the two sobbing women at his feet. "Ramon's wife and daughter." He kicked the mother, forcing her to land on her side on the hay, moaning when he struck her right in the rib cage.

I'd seen my father do worse, so I wasn't surprised by his cruelty—but I was surprised by his insanity. "And what are you going to do to them?"

"Exactly what Ramon did to my wife."

My jaw almost dropped to the floor. "Father..."

"His daughter is quite pretty." He looked down at her, a girl who couldn't be a day older than twenty. "And young. You'll take her. Ramon will watch as we rape and torture his family."

Jesus fucking Christ. "Have you lost your fucking mind?"

He walked over to the door where Ramon was locked away. He used his key to open it and then swung the door outward.

Ramon took one look at his family and sprinted.

My father slugged him in the stomach then forced him back. "Move, and I'll kill them both."

Ramon collapsed against the wall, horrified by the sight.

My father grabbed both of the women and dragged them into the cell.

Ramon immediately clutched both of them and cradled them into his side even though he was powerless to protect them from my father's menace. "Caspian, don't do this. Do whatever you want to me, but don't—"

"Don't what?" My father stepped farther into the cell. "Don't rape your wife? The way you raped mine?"

Ramon shut his mouth, knowing he couldn't argue with the words that flew out of my father's mouth.

"Don't rape your daughter?" my father asked. "The way your men raped my wife? My son will take her first, and then my men will take her. When they're both begging for death, I'll torture them and hang them in this very barn—so you can watch their corpses rot in the Tuscan heat." He backed out of the barn.

"Caspian, listen to me!" Ramon struggled to his feet. "I'll give you whatever—"

My father turned around. "The one thing I want is my wife. Give her to me, and we'll call this whole thing off."

Ramon breathed with his panic, his face covered in sweat as he tried to think of a solution to this problem, to spare his wife and daughter from gruesome deaths. But money couldn't fix this problem. Nothing could fix this problem.

My father grabbed the door. "That's right...you killed her." He slammed the door then locked it. "Enjoy your last night with your family. We begin tomorrow." Sobs sounded from the door as the women started to heave in terror. As if nothing had happened, my father brushed it off and walked toward the barn doors.

My eyes followed him before my feet did the same. "You can't be serious."

"I am." He pushed the doors open then approached his truck. "He gets exactly what he deserves."

I wanted justice for Mom as much as he did, but I knew she wouldn't want this. She wouldn't want us to hurt two innocent people. "It won't make you feel better. It won't make losing Mom easier."

He turned around, flashing me another look of disappointment. "I thought this was the one thing we were united on. Now you're telling me you're a coward."

"I'm not a coward. I just don't want to rape someone." Just when I thought my father couldn't get any worse, he did. Just when I thought he couldn't be crueler, he was. He'd completely lost his sense of humanity.

"I don't want to rape those women either, but we have to."

"But we don't." I threw down my arms. "Mom wouldn't want this. Yes, she would want you to kill Ramon but not hurt his family. They had nothing to do with this."

"And neither did she." He'd already made up his mind, and he wasn't going to change it. He displayed the coldness of a statue that stood in the snow, his expression permanent.

"Ramon didn't touch me or Lily."

"But Lily is a lunatic in a mental institution, and my son is a coward."

"She's not in a mental institution…she's in rehab."

"Whatever." It didn't matter; he couldn't care less. "We're doing this."

"I'm not." I didn't care if my father hated me forever, but I wasn't going to rape someone. I wasn't a good man, but I wasn't evil either. Plus, I had absolutely no desire to force a woman to do anything. I got more pussy than I could handle. "And you think Mom would want you to fuck someone? Rape someone?"

"It doesn't matter what she wants. I need Ramon to suffer the way that I suffered."

"But it won't change anything!" I threw down my arms again. "Mom is dead, and she's not coming back. This rampage isn't healing your wounds. It's making them bigger, making them fester." Now I understood why he didn't torture Ramon right away. Even before he captured him, my father knew he was going to take Ramon's family—and he didn't tell me because he knew I would never approve.

Once again, my father looked at me like I was worthless. "Fine. I have plenty of men who would be happy to oblige. I shouldn't have depended on you in the first place."

"Yes…you shouldn't have depended on me to rape some-one." My mother would roll in her grave if she knew I did something like that. She would be screaming right now if she knew my father had taken this so far. "Don't do this. Please. I didn't marry Arwen so we could rape and murder innocent people." I'd never begged someone to do anything, but my pride couldn't stop me from doing it now.

He opened the door to his truck and turned back to look at me. "Get in my way, and I'll kill you—and your wife."

ARWEN

AFTER I FINISHED MY PERFORMANCE AT THE OPERA, I CHANGED my clothes in the dressing room then slipped out the back to head to my car in the rear of the building. The street was usually deserted, and there was plenty of parking because it was designated for staff only. With my keys in hand, I approached my black Mercedes.

"Arwen." A deep voice sounded behind me, masculine and authoritative.

I knew it wasn't Maverick, but I turned around to size up the man who followed me. He held flowers in his hand, lilies and roses, and he wore a collared shirt and slacks, like he'd been in the audience just minutes ago. To top it off, he was handsome.

He smiled at me before he came closer. "Okay, I know this looks super creepy, so let me explain. I asked the stage guys to give these to you, but they said you'd already left. I got your name from the program they hand out. That's how I ended up here...chasing you in the dark like a weirdo."

He seemed so normal, I realized. Something I wasn't used to.

"I wanted you to have these. You put on quite the show."

"Thank you." I took the flowers from him, and automatically, I smelled them. "They're beautiful."

"And I was hoping I could ask you out...even though I see that beautiful diamond on your left hand. I'm not the kind of guy that normally goes for married women, but you kinda stole my obsession the moment I saw you."

I never took my ring off unless I was home. Now it was an extension of me, a piece of jewelry I flaunted because I loved it...even though it didn't actually mean anything. "My husband and I have an open relationship..." I wouldn't give him the specifics because it was a secret I needed to hide.

"That works out nicely for me. So, can I take you to dinner?"

I would love to walk to a restaurant together and share a bottle of wine, a spur-of-the-moment meeting with a handsome stranger. My entire life was ahead of me, and anything could happen. If only I were unattached, I could really enjoy it. "I can't really be in public. How about we order a pizza and go to your place?"

His grin widened, like the suggestion was better than the one he'd had. "Perfect."

THE SEX WAS GOOD. It was unplanned and spontaneous, and the mystery was so exciting that it made the sex better than it really was. This handsome man could be anyone, a long-term lover or maybe the man I'd fall in love with.

Maverick gave me hope that I could still have all of my dreams. When enough time passed, we could drop the charade and sign the divorce papers so we could go our separate ways. I could get married the right way. Fall in love with someone first—and then vow to love him for the rest of my life.

I had to admit that sex with Maverick was better. He was bigger, more dominant, and he could kiss more masterfully than anyone else. But that was just casual sex between two friends—and it meant nothing to either one of us.

I lay in bed next to Henry, his naked body wrapped around mine. He had dirty-blond hair and blue eyes, completely different from Maverick in every way. He was strong and muscular, but he didn't have that chiseled physique I was used to.

Henry ran his fingers down my back. "Sleep over."

Maverick was under the impression I was coming home, and I needed to tell him if my plans had changed. If I didn't at least text him, he would blow up my phone with a vengeance. He didn't care where I went or who I slept with. He just wanted to know where I was and when I would be coming home. "Let me call my husband and let him know."

His eyes narrowed slightly, clearly surprised by the mechanics of my marriage. "Wow, you guys are really open."

"Yeah...we're good friends."

"If you were my wife, I wouldn't share you with anybody." He leaned over and kissed my neck and shoulder, devouring me with anxious lips.

I wanted to stay and let the kisses continue, but if I didn't make that call now, I never would. Then Maverick would scream at me. "I'll be right back." I slid out of bed, grabbed my phone, and walked into the living room. I paced the floor buck naked. I held the phone to my ear and listened to it ring.

He answered after a couple of rings. "Everything alright?" His voice deep and menacing, Maverick somehow sounded angry all the time. He was irritable and cold, making him somewhat heartless. He cared about some things, but he was so stony that he refused to care about other things. But tonight, he seemed particularly flustered.

"Yeah. I just wanted to tell you that I won't be home until tomorrow. I met someone."

Dead silent.

I expected him to brush off my announcement like it didn't matter, but he was so quiet on the other end, it seemed like he'd hung up. "Is that okay...?"

"It's fine." He spat out the words harshly, like it was anything but fine.

It didn't make sense. He'd just given a long speech about how I would never mean anything to him, how the sex would be casual and nothing more. But now he seemed so angry, he was seething. "What's wrong?"

"Nothing."

Living with this man had taught me so much about his composure, about the way his tone changed when something was on his mind. I also could read his expressions well, know when he was trying to keep me at a distance so I wouldn't discover his secrets. "It's not nothing. Now, tell me."

"Goodnight, Arwen." He hung up.

I listened to the line go dead, having no idea what Maverick was so upset about. It couldn't be me. He couldn't possibly be jealous or possessive. That meant it was something else...maybe something important.

I walked back into the bedroom. "I can't stay tonight. I'm sorry."

He groaned. "That's too bad. Another time, then?"

"Sure. That sounds good." I picked up my clothes off the ground and started to dress.

"Did your husband realize he was making a mistake letting you sleep with another man?"

"No. He's pissed about something else and refuses to tell me what it is." I pulled on my dress then slipped on my heels. "So I'm going to drag it out of him. Sometimes, men can be so difficult...and my husband is the most difficult man I know."

I MADE it to the third floor and noticed his office door was open.

He was sitting at his desk, a bottle of scotch beside him without a glass, and his lips rested against his joined fingers. His eyes were closed, as if he were ignoring a migraine or thinking about something particularly disturbing.

I stepped inside, my heels announcing my presence.

He lifted his chin from his fingers and looked at me, the surprise on his face showing he clearly hadn't been expecting me to walk through the door. His brown eyes were full of malice, and if that bottle had been new, he'd drunk half of it on his own. He stared at me for a moment before his gaze shifted away. "Why are you here?"

I moved to the couch and slipped off my heels. "Because you're pissed about something."

"I'm always pissed."

With my heels off, I got back to my feet and approached

his desk. "No, you aren't." I grabbed the bottle and dragged it toward me. "Now, tell me what's bothering you."

"You should have stayed in bed with your boyfriend." He leaned back in his chair, putting distance between us when I came too close. The only time he did that was when he was truly bothered by something.

"He's not my boyfriend. And you're more important." I took a drink straight from the bottle then returned it to his desk.

He continued to watch me, rage in his eyes.

"Don't worry. I won't drink it all." I scooted the bottle closer to him. "I'm here now, so you may as well tell me what's going on. I can tell you're angry by the way your shoulders are hunched, by the dismissive tone in your voice. We agreed we were friends—and friends tell each other stuff."

He watched me for a long time, still as a statue. He rose to his feet unexpectedly, his physical fitness giving him the grace to move quickly and fluidly. He grabbed the bottle off the desk as he made his way to one of the couches.

I sat across from him, just as I did when we first smoked and drank together.

He took another drink before he set it down. When his elbows rested on his knees and his body hunched forward, his clothes tightened against his powerful frame, showing how strong he was. If anyone else moved like that, it would only highlight their flaws. His hands rubbed together, the veins on his hands protruding from his tanned skin.

I waited for him to speak his mind, to tell me what troubled him so much.

"My father has completely lost his mind...and I don't

know what to do about it. I don't think there *is* anything I can do about it."

My father had been the beacon in my life, the foundation under my feet. A day never went by when I didn't know he loved me. But Maverick's relationship with his own father couldn't be more different.

He took another drink then rubbed the side of his head with his palm, rubbing the aches and pains away.

"What did he do?"

With his eyes downcast, he shook his head slightly, like he didn't want to say. "Ramon captured my mom, raped her, tortured her, and then killed her. That was why my father wanted Ramon so much...to give my mother justice."

This was all old news to me, but I stayed patient and kept quiet.

"I thought it was strange my father kept Ramon in the barn for so long. He's been in there for almost a week..."

It was strange. Caspian worked so hard to capture that man, but once he had him, he abandoned him.

"But it all made sense when I went to the barn this afternoon." Maverick still couldn't look at me, like it was too difficult to meet my gaze and get the words out. "My father captured Ramon's wife and daughter...and intends to rape and torture them."

When the words fell on my ears, I finally understood why Maverick was so disturbed. His father lacked a heart or a conscience, but this was surprising, even for him. "What...?"

"The daughter is about twenty. He told me to rape her while he raped the mother." He dragged his hands over his face like the conversation had scarred him.

"You can't be serious." Ramon's actions were inexcusable.

He deserved to be butchered into pieces. But his wife and daughter...they had nothing to do with this. "Those women probably had no idea Ramon did that to your mother. They're no different than a stranger on the street. He can't do this."

"I know...that's what I said to him. When I refused to rape the girl, he looked at me like I'd stabbed him in the back." He dropped his hands and grabbed the bottle again. "He said his men will step up and do what I can't..." He took another drink, this time a much bigger gulp.

This man was evil. "Who the hell tells their son to rape someone?"

He stared at the bottle, his gaze lifeless. "Told you... It's a fucking nightmare. My mother wouldn't want this. I told him that, but he won't listen. I told him it wouldn't make him feel better, but he didn't listen to that either."

"Where are they now?"

"Locked in the barn with Ramon. My father wanted them to be together for one more day...just to make it worse when he takes the women away."

I understood he was a grieving man who'd lost the love of his life, but this was insane. "You can't let him do that, Maverick." Those two women were just people who were in the wrong place at the wrong time.

"I tried to talk him out of it."

"Well, try again." How could I sit by when those two women would be tortured tomorrow? "I understand why Ramon has to die. He should die. But his wife and daughter didn't do anything wrong."

"I agree, but my father doesn't see it that way. Ramon tortured his wife, so he wants to torture his."

"That doesn't make it right." I couldn't keep my voice down. Slowly, it rose higher and higher.

"I know."

"And Ramon didn't touch you or your sister, so why did your father drag Ramon's daughter into this?"

He shook his head. "Because he's a psychopath."

"You have to do something, Maverick. You can't just sit there and turn the other cheek. These women are going to be raped and tortured to death. It's not right."

He bowed his head. "I don't have any options."

"Yes, you do. Take them out of the barn. This is your property."

"It's a legacy property. He still has some ownership over the place."

"Whatever," I hissed. "Free them. Get them out of here."

He lifted his chin to look at me. "There's nothing I can do. My father can't see reason when it comes to this. If I break them out of the barn and make it look like they broke out themselves, he'll just hunt them down again. If I free them myself, he'll hunt them down again. There's nothing I can do. His mind is made up, and he's not going to change it."

"So, you just give up?" I asked sadly. "Those are innocent people…"

"Not once have I said I'm a good guy. I'm not the hero who saves the damsel in distress. I don't think these women deserve what's coming to them, but I'm not going to get killed for their sake. If Ramon really gave a damn about protecting his family, he wouldn't go making enemies with people like my father. He didn't have to rape and murder my mother. That was his decision, and he has to live with it."

I would never make a case for Ramon's defense, but his

wife and daughter were a different story. "Your mother wouldn't want this…"

"But she's not here," he said bitterly. "It doesn't matter what she would want."

"It does matter. You can't let him get away with this."

Both of his hands balled into fists, like he was losing his temper. "The only way I can stop this from happening is by killing my father. I hate the son of a bitch with a passion, but I don't want to pop a couple of bullets into his skull. So, do you have a better idea?"

I sat there with dread in my heart, knowing I couldn't come up with a plan that would fix the problem. I'd seen Caspian with my own eyes and understood how distorted his sense of reality was. Even if Maverick managed to help these women, Caspian would hunt them down again. Their only chance of survival was to return to wherever they were from, and Ramon's men could protect them. Somehow, Caspian had kidnapped them the first time, but it would be nearly impossible to do it a second time.

When I didn't say anything, he sighed. "It's not right, but there's nothing anyone can do. My father has his mind made up, and nothing will change it. I say we just forget about it…" He grabbed the neck of the bottle and rested it on his thigh.

I knew Maverick had a much different perspective of himself. He considered himself cold and cruel, the spitting image of his father. But if that were true, he wouldn't be trying to drink his sorrows away, to repress the memories because they were too hard to bear. It was killing him inside to know this was happening…because he cared.

There were a few things I didn't like about his character, but the more I got to know him, the more I respected him. He was cruel in his own way, but he was also extremely kind... and generous. He'd been my rock since the beginning, the support I leaned on to get through the day. Our marriage was a sham, but I relied on him the way every wife relied on her husband.

Why didn't his father see him the same way? Not as a disappointment...but as a good man he should be proud of.

PINNING the flashlight between my neck and shoulder, I focused the light on the door so I could grab the handle and slide it open. It was three in the morning, and the sky was so dark that stars and planets were Christmas lights that blanketed the sky. I pushed inside and saw the piles of hay on the ground.

All the doors to the stalls were open—except one.

There were hooks drilled into the wall, a place to hang keys. There was only one set, so I assumed that was what I needed. I grabbed them then moved to the door, my footsteps loud against the hay underneath my feet.

Their bodies stirred on the other side. "Dad..." The woman whispered to her father as she heard me slip the key in the door.

"It's happening." Another female voice entered the silence.

The second I opened this door, Ramon could overpower me. I didn't have a weapon, and if I let Ramon go, then that wouldn't be right. I wasn't a fan of violence, but he needed to be punished for what he had done. So I couldn't let him... only the women. "My name is Arwen. Maverick is my husband. He told me what's supposed to happen in the morning."

They were silent, not moving or breathing.

"I don't think it's right. I think Caspian is taking it too far. So, I want to let you go...but I have to make a deal with you first."

"Please let us go." The older woman turned aggressive, slamming her fists into the door. "Please. At least let my daughter go."

Listening to them was just as bad as the horror I imagined. "I'll let you both go...but Ramon has to stay. I don't have a weapon, so I can't keep you inside this cell once I open it." Maybe being honest wasn't the best way to go. He might just break down the door, kill me, and then run off. "So you have to make a deal with me. When I open the door, you stay put...and let the women go. If you give me any reason to doubt you, I'll just go back to the house now. So, you need to decide what kind of man you want to be. Do you want to save your wife and daughter? Or do you want to be a coward?"

They whispered to one another, their voices barely audible.

It didn't take long for them to make a decision. Ramon spoke next. "Please save my family..."

I could hear the sincerity in his voice, the way it cracked with emotion. I could hear his beating heart, his gratitude. It was just a single sentence, but it conveyed so much. "Alright..." I turned the key and opened the door.

Ramon was hugging both of them, letting his wife cry against his chest while his daughter whimpered. "I love you." He kissed each one on the head. "Both of you." Despite the barbaric thing he had done, he was still a man...someone with feelings and a breaking heart.

It was almost too hard to watch.

The daughter came out first, followed by the mother a moment later. Both had tears streaming down their faces, knowing this was the last time they would ever see him.

I started to shut the door again.

Ramon pressed his palm against the wood, keeping it steady.

I tensed, afraid I'd just fallen into his trap. He was much bigger than I was, a thousand times stronger.

"Thank you..." He held my gaze before he dropped his hand and allowed the door to close.

I locked it and put the key back on the hook.

"Now what?" The mother had her arm around her daughter, her eyes puffy with tears.

"I'm gonna put you in the trunk of my car and drive you out of here. Then you can keep the car and drive wherever you want to go."

She stared at me in disbelief, as if she couldn't believe a stranger would do such a thing. "Why are you doing this?"

My answer was simple. "Because it's the right thing to do."

I woke up late that morning since I'd snuck out of the house in the middle of the night. I didn't get back into bed until nearly five. By the time I woke up, it was way past breakfast time. I made my downstairs and hoped I could get any early lunch.

Flashbacks of the previous night came back to me, of

driving out of the gate while security watched me strangely. When I made it to the road, I popped the trunk and handed over the keys. Both women hugged me because they were so grateful.

Then I'd walked back to the gate and returned to the house.

When I entered the dining room, Maverick was still there. Normally, he'd be at work right now, but he sat in front of his mug of coffee like he'd been there for hours. Dressed in a black t-shirt and jeans, he looked casual, his plans for the day unclear.

I lowered myself into the chair and filled my mug with coffee.

Maverick's eyes were still directed out the window, the espresso color of his gaze matching the contents of his cup. His jawline was smooth from a morning shave, but a hint of a shadow was still visible because his hair grew back the second he swiped his razor over the area. It was a beautiful summer day, and the brightness outside reflected in his cold eyes. He didn't turn to look at me, either ignoring me or so focused that he didn't notice I had joined him.

There was some leftover toast, so I smeared the jam across the cold piece of bread. The coffee was barely warm too, but since I was so late, I didn't complain. After the long night I'd had, I was hungrier than usual. Running around all night caused me to work up an appetite.

Minutes later, he finally turned his gaze back to me.

With the subtlest expression, he could show his rage so well. His chest rose and fell at a slightly rapid rate because he was livid. His eyes broadcast his fury because he hadn't blinked once since I'd joined him. Now he looked at me like I wasn't a friend, a lover, or his wife. He looked at me like he'd just marked me as the enemy. "You let them go, didn't you?"

I knew security would notify him when I returned to the estate on foot in the middle of the night. The car was gone, and I had no explanation for what happened to it. Foolishly, I thought there was a chance I'd gotten away with it when he didn't break down my bedroom door to choke me.

He continued to stare at me as if he was expecting an answer.

That look was so terrifying that I broke eye contact and looked into my cup.

His gaze was still searing hot. "You gave them your car and let them get away."

I drank from my mug, feeling like a child who was avoiding the terrifying expression of a parent. I was too scared to look up, too scared to face whatever punishment he would give me. He'd never laid a hand on me or made me feel unsafe, but he'd never used that tone of voice with me either.

"Look. At. Me."

I lowered my mug then finally lifted my gaze to meet his.

Now, he was even more livid. "You told me we were allies. Allies don't stab each other in the back like this."

"I didn't stab you—"

"Shut your mouth. I'm talking—you're listening."

The only reason I listened was because I felt so guilty about what I'd done.

With wide eyes and a promise of violence in his limbs, he looked at me like I was the sheep he was about to slaughter—not protect. "You're my wife, and you're supposed to obey me. How dare you go behind my back and do this? You have no idea what you're doing. You have no idea what game you're playing. You're supposed to be loyal to me and no one else. This is a violation of that trust. And once trust is broken, it can never be mended."

I swiped my tongue across my lips, my heart hammering a million miles a minute. I had to save those women, but I also felt terrible for how much I'd upset him. "I didn't mean to—"

"What did I say?"

I shut my mouth again.

"This is why I don't trust anyone. You let your guard down for a goddamn second, and shit happens."

His words hurt me far more than I expected. I didn't want him to think I was disloyal to him, that my decision had anything to do with our relationship. There was so much pain in my chest, heartbreak that came from an unidentified source. Knowing I hurt him hurt me. Knowing I made him regret trusting him killed me. This relationship was the only good thing I had in my life. He was the only man I could depend on. "Maverick, please..."

He raised his hand, and that was enough to shut me up. "You have no idea what you've done. You have no idea the consequences I'm about to face. If letting them go in the middle of the night was such a simple solution, I would have done it. You're a stupid girl who doesn't understand how the real world works. You're a liability that I now have to pay for—"

The sound of the front door flying open and slamming against the wall reached down the hallway and entered our ears. It was such a loud explosion, like a car crashing into a brick wall.

I flinched in my chair.

Maverick didn't react at all, like he'd been waiting for the sound. "Leave. Now." He stayed in his chair, his eyes averted as he listened to the sound of marching footsteps approaching the dining room. He was calm but tense at the same time, his back turned to whoever was approaching. "Don't make me ask you again."

I listened because that was what he wanted. I got out of my chair and headed to the staircase.

Caspian entered the room a moment later, looking twice as tall when he was furious. His eyes were wider than I'd ever seen them, and invisible flames burned from all of his limbs as he stormed into the house.

Maverick rose from his chair and faced him, moving with calmness despite the wrath he was confronted with.

Caspian stopped in front of him, looking at his son like he wanted to shoot him right between the eyes.

I should keep moving up the stairs, but I stayed, watching the way Caspian showed all of his rage in just a single look. The loathing was paramount, the hatred profound.

Caspian turned still as a statue, but it was just a pause before the storm. "You are so fucking worthless." Spit flew out of his mouth because he was shaking from head to toe. Hands balled into fists. Eyebrows furrowed. "Your mother would hate you as much as I hate you. I've never been more disgusted with my own bloodline. My wife gave me a son to carry on my name, but she gave me a coward I wish had never been born."

Jesus Christ.

Maverick took the abuse without blinking, appearing oddly calm despite the insults thrown in his face.

Caspian launched his attack an instant later, slamming his fist into Maverick's face. Despite his age, he packed so much force into the hit and forced Maverick back. The movement was so quick that I couldn't see it coming.

Maverick fell back from the momentum of the blow and crashed into the hardwood floor.

Caspian stood over him and kicked him hard in the ribs. "I'm gonna drag you outside and hang you just way Ramon hung your mother. I'm gonna watch the life disappear from your eyes as you gasp for air like a drowning rat." He kicked him again.

I covered my mouth, my eyes watering.

Caspian grabbed Maverick's neck with both hands and started to squeeze, a maniacal gleam in his eyes. He pressed his fingers into his skin and cut off his air supply. "You would die for those whores? You would rather let them go and betray your family than honor your mother's memory? Where did I go wrong with you?"

Maverick didn't seem to be fighting back, like he'd lost the will to live. Listening to his father threaten to kill him probably sucked the life out of him, probably disturbed him so much that he didn't have any drive to win the battle. It was easier just to give up than to live with a father that hated him.

Caspian wasn't stopping.

Maverick had given up.

But I couldn't let him throw in the towel. "It wasn't him. I was the one who let them go." I moved to the bottom of the stairs, gripping the handrail for balance because I knew something terrible was about to happen. I didn't have a gun or a knife, and the dining table was too far away.

Caspian's head popped up, and he looked at me as he kept choking his son.

Life came back into Maverick's eyes when he heard the words fly out of my mouth. He'd been still just a moment ago, but now his hands reached up to grab his father's wrists.

"Maverick had nothing to do with it." My fingers tightened on the wood. "I told Maverick to let them go, but he refused. So I snuck out in the middle of the night, released them, and hid them in the trunk of my car as I snuck them outside the gate." I wouldn't stand by and let Maverick be punished for my betrayal. Even if I didn't survive what was to come next, I didn't care.

He released Maverick's throat then rose to his feet, those brown eyes focused on me like I was prey.

Maverick heaved on the ground, gasping for air because he'd been without it for over a minute. He grabbed his throat and sucked the air into his lungs, clearly on the verge of passing out.

Caspian took a step toward me, his gaze darkening like a billowing cloud in the distance. Heavy with rain, it was about to drop on both of us, a storm unlike any other. His eyes narrowed as the blood lust filled his gaze.

I knew I was going to die.

He took another step toward me then pulled a knife out of his pocket.

Shit.

Maverick continued to heave on the floor, his body and mind disabled.

I took a step back, moving up the stairs.

Caspian gripped the knife and watched me with the same stare his son possessed. Eyes color of coffee and filled with the same rage, he looked like a butcher about to slice me into pieces. He didn't blink, not once since his attention had been directed on me.

I was in a bad spot, backed up onto a staircase. There was nowhere for me to run, and this man was probably much faster. If he couldn't reach me, he could just throw the knife at me and kill me instantly.

"If you think you're safe because of the deal your father made with me, you're wrong. The contract became null the second you betrayed my son, betrayed me. I will gut you like a fish and leave your body on your father's grave."

I could have kept my mouth shut and let Maverick suffer the consequences, but I couldn't live with that guilt. Maverick was a man I respected, even if he pissed me off sometimes, and I didn't want him to suffer at the hands of his father for another second. The thought made me oddly calm, chased away the fear that caused my anxiety. I could try to run, but I wouldn't get far. I'd rather die with a knife in my front from fighting than one in my back from running. "Instead of focusing on what you've lost—"

He didn't listen to a word I said and used my speech as a distraction. He sprinted at me, about to reach the first step and lodge that knife into my belly. He moved at an incredible speed, like he was a man still vibrant in his youth.

My instincts kicked in, and I screamed.

Caspian fell to the ground and dropped the knife, stopping just inches from me.

I fell back, unable to keep my balance with all the mayhem.

Maverick had managed to lunge forward and grab him by

the ankle. He yanked on his body and dragged him away from the knife.

Caspian kicked him away then crawled toward the knife again.

Maverick was no longer submissive. He jumped to his feet and yanked his father back, dragging him across the floor so the knife was out of reach. "Stop it."

"You little..." Caspian rolled onto his back and then climbed to his feet, slamming his fist into Maverick's face. "How dare you defend that whore?"

Maverick blocked the hit then punched his father in the face.

Caspian fell back, clearly shocked that his own son had hit him. He wiped away the blood dripping from his nose onto his fingertips then looked back at him, appalled. "You choose her over me?"

Maverick maneuvered to the stairs, his hands up and ready for a fight. Now his body stood in the way, protecting me so Caspian couldn't get to me. "You need to calm down."

"Calm down?" He dropped his bloody hand, his voice rising in offense. "She took away the one thing that mattered to me." He inched closer. "I worked my ass off for that. Your mother deserves justice—"

"That's not justice, Father. It's sick. Mom wouldn't want that, and you know she wouldn't. You've lost your goddamn mind, and you're so twisted, you can't even see it. Arwen didn't want those two women to suffer when they didn't deserve it. She can think clearly—you can't."

He stepped closer. "After everything I've done for you, this is how you treat me?"

"What have you done for me?" Maverick continued to

place his body in front of me, lining up his frame so he protected me at all times. "When Mom died, you died too. You're a ghost of the man you used to be. I used to be proud of you, used to look up to you. But now you're heartless, hateful of everyone in this world because you lost the one person you loved. Lily and I don't matter—"

Caspian lunged at Maverick, slamming his large body into his frame and landing a punch against his jaw. He used all of his energy to cause as much damage as possible, to make Maverick bleed and hurt.

Maverick took a few hits because he was shocked by his father's savage attack. He fell back, his head about to hit the corner of the bottom stair.

Even though it would hurt, I fell and slid my body underneath him, using my thighs as a cushion so he wouldn't crack his head open and bleed everywhere. But that put me in line with Caspian, easily accessible.

Caspian took advantage of my position and grabbed me by the neck, squeezing me so hard I couldn't breathe right from the beginning.

Maverick recovered quickly and kicked his father off. Punch after punch, he planted his fists into his father's body, turning into a beast with enough adrenaline to power a rocket. He slammed his fists into his father's face and his stomach, driving him back to the other side of the room. Caspian's face was battered by the time he collapsed on the ground, breathing hard as his son stood over him, blood on his knuckles.

Caspian raised his gaze and looked at his son, blood dripping from his mouth and his nose. Bruised and swollen, his face looked like he'd been stung by a swarm of hornets. He leaned against the wall as he looked at his son with pure disgust.

Maverick was still, waiting for his father's next move.

Caspian slowly rose to his feet, finally showing the effect his age had on his body. He didn't carry himself with strength, but defeat. But the look he gave his son showed the promise of war, of torture, of bloodlust. He sent Maverick a cold stare, as if he might continue the fight even if he lost. But then he turned around and walked off, moving with a slight limp and sagging shoulders.

Maverick held his position until his father was out of the house. He looked through the window and watched him get into his car and drive away. Once he was really gone, he released the breath he was holding and turned to me.

Now he looked even more furious with me.

Like he blamed me for everything.

23

MAVERICK

I SAT IN MY OFFICE WITH A CIGAR IN MY MOUTH, absentmindedly puffing the smoke and letting it disappear from my mouth. There was a painting on the other side of the wall, of Paris in the early 1800s before it became industrialized. It was moody and dark, showing the mud after a bad storm. I didn't pick out most of my artwork, but I'd chosen this one because it spoke to me.

I stared at it now, doing my best to think about nothing.

My neck was visibly bruised because of the way my father had strangled me. My face was tinted from the fists I took to the face. I looked like I'd gotten my ass kicked even though my father got the worst of it.

It was the only time I'd ever struck my father.

I didn't feel good about it—even though I didn't have a choice.

If I did nothing, he would have killed Arwen... Not that I should care.

She betrayed me, after all.

When my cigar burned out, I lit another one.

Didn't give a shit if I got cancer.

My father and I didn't have a good relationship, but this made us complete enemies. Now I had two wars to fight. I had to make sure Kamikaze didn't come near Arwen, and I had to make sure my father didn't kill her either.

Or did I?

My father was right when he said she breached the contract. She defied our wishes and took matters into her own hands. That was direct disobedience. I had every right to leave her.

Maybe I should.

The door opened, and she appeared in the doorway, apology in her eyes and concern in her stature. She searched my gaze for permission to enter the room.

She wouldn't get it from me.

She stepped inside anyway and approached my desk, her hands together in a timid fashion. She was in jeans and a t-shirt, her dark hair pulled over one shoulder. Her face was free of makeup because she'd probably spent all afternoon thinking about the shit that had happened earlier in the day.

The longer I stared at her, the angrier I became.

She stared at the cigar in my hand, like she was too ashamed to meet my gaze. She kept her look there for nearly a minute before her eyes lifted to look into mine. Her blue gaze conveyed her sorrow, her obvious regret. "Maverick...I'm so sorry." She took a deep breath like the words made her chest clench in pain.

Those words meant nothing to me.

"I wasn't thinking. I just—"

"No, you weren't." I puffed on my cigar again.

"I just couldn't let those women be tortured..."

"This is how I know you're stupid." I pulled the cigar out of my mouth and let the remaining smoke rise from my mouth as I spoke. "You have no grasp of an ecosystem. My father and I live in the same system. You manipulate one aspect, and it changes everything that surrounds it. You saved those two women—but now my father and I are enemies. You took away the one thing that mattered to him, and now he won't stop until he kills you—and me."

Her eyes dropped in regret.

"I want a divorce." His voice was cold.

When her eyes lifted again, there was true terror in her gaze, like the idea of losing me was more than she could stand. She knew she needed me for everything, from shelter to protection. Without me, she was nothing.

I waited for her to argue, to beg me to change my mind.

But she didn't. "Would that help the situation with you and your father?"

No, it probably wouldn't make a difference. I smoked my cigar again.

When she knew I wouldn't answer her, she didn't press me. "I understand..."

The second I kicked her out of my house, the dogs would descend. Kamikaze would grab her and turn her into a slave, unless my father got to her first. He would just kill her, shoot her between the eyes. If I were her, I'd hope to run into my father first.

She stared down at her fingers as she gripped the edge of the desk. "I'm sorry, Maverick. I don't regret saving those women, but I regret what I put you through. You don't deserve to be treated like that by your own father. I know I'm the one to blame for this...but your father is the one who needs help. His response to the situation shouldn't have been violence. He shouldn't have marched to his son's door with the intention of killing him. I know I triggered these events…but he's the one who's wrong."

"That's not how the real world works."

"I know, but you should consider talking to your father. He clearly needs help…and he's only becoming crazier."

He became more barbaric every time I saw him. "Take the cash I gave you and go."

She froze. "I gave it to the women…so they could disappear."

This just kept getting worse and worse. "I'm not giving you another penny."

"I wasn't going to ask."

"Good. Get out." I didn't want to see her ever again. I wanted this liability out of my house.

She lingered at my desk, her eyes downcast. Without me, she had nothing—and she knew it. In that moment, she probably understood she'd thrown away a great thing. She probably understood how much I did for her, how much I protected her. But my kindness had expired, and there was nothing she could do about it. "I'll leave in the morning."

I was hoping she would leave now, but I would take it.

She was still rooted to her spot in front of my desk. "When my father told me I had to marry you, I was furious. My whole life had been taken from me. But as I got to know you, I realized you were a good man…with a big heart. I started to care for you, admire you. I even started to see you as my friend. I'm sorry I betrayed you. That was never my intention. I just wanted to do the right thing. I didn't realize how much it would cost you…and I apologize for that."

Heartlessly, I stared at her with the burning cigar between my fingertips.

She waited another moment to see if I would say anything. But when I didn't, she gave up and turned away. "Goodbye, Maverick."

I watched her walk out the door, both disappointed and relieved by her departure. "Goodbye, Sheep."

———

LILY SAT across from me at the table in the dining hall. Other members of the rehab facility chatted with family members over dinner, pretending everything was normal even though they were battling addiction.

Lily took a few bites of her dinner but left most of it untouched. She was a pretty woman, but she looked sickly with the amount of weight she'd lost. She used to have beautiful, thick hair, but now it had thinned out from lack of nutrition. Her skin didn't glow the way it used to. Now it looked just as pale as her eyes. "How are things with you?"

"Not good." I hadn't visited her in a while, which made me feel guilty. It made me feel even guiltier because I only came tonight because I needed someone to talk to. But then again, she forgot my birthday, so we were even.

"What's wrong?"

I told her everything that had happened with Father.

Lily's lifeless expression instantly changed. Horrified by every single aspect of the story, she was agitated. "What the hell is wrong with him? He's even worse than I realized. How could Mom's death make him so psychotic?"

I didn't have an answer, and I was tired of guessing. "I'm divorcing her."

Lily stared at me, her food abandoned and her eyebrow raised. "Why?"

"I can't be married to someone I don't trust."

"You didn't know her when you married her, so you obviously didn't trust her then."

But things had changed since our wedding day.

"What about the men who are after her? Won't they get her?"

"Not my problem."

"And you're just okay with that?" she asked incredulously.

"If she wanted to stay married to me, she shouldn't have betrayed me."

"She didn't betray you," Lily argued. "She wanted to save those women, and I can't fault her for that. How could Father possibly think that's okay? You were okay turning the other cheek while those women were tortured?"

"No, but I didn't have any other choice."

"Well, Arwen obviously couldn't live with that...and I don't blame her. She obviously wasn't aware of the repercussions at the time, but she did the right thing. Mom would be happy if she knew what Arwen did."

Maybe. We would never know.

"Maverick, if you leave her, she'll be raped and tortured too. You're really okay with that?"

Arwen was a strong woman who didn't take shit from anyone, but Kamikaze was a mutant. With his almost seven feet of height, she would have no chance against him—and he would probably be the first one to fuck her. She'd be subjected to a life she didn't want, a life that made death preferable. And if Kamikaze didn't get her first, then my father would...and he would execute her.

"I know you're upset right now, but leaving her isn't an option. You couldn't live with yourself if something terrible happened to her. She didn't betray you for her own gain. She did it to save those innocent people. Cut her some slack."

"Now Father and I are enemies...and I should just forgive her?"

"You're enemies because Father is batshit crazy. At some point in time, shit was going to hit the fan anyway. He's so unstable that he can't even think logically. Who kidnaps innocent women to rape them? And then who tries to murder their own son for saving them? He's the problem—not her."

I stared at the food, recognizing her clear logic.

"Honestly, I like this girl...and I think you do too."

"I never said I liked her."

"You said she broke your trust, which meant you trusted her in the first place. That's impossible for someone like you."

I hated the fact that my little sister was smarter than me.

"And if you trusted her at any point, she must mean something to you."

I didn't know what Arwen meant to me. I liked fucking her. I considered her to be a friend. When it came down to it, I'd picked her over my father and saved her life. It would have been easy for me to let him kill her. It would have fixed all my problems. But I'd protected her, not because of my promise, but because I wanted to.

Lily kept watching me. "Go home to your wife, Maverick. And hope that she's still there."

24

ARWEN

I took the clothes Maverick paid for because he had no use for them. I may as well keep them, especially since my wardrobe was limited. All of my stuff fit in a single suitcase—reminding me how insignificant I was.

Once I was outside the gates, I had no idea what I would do.

I had nowhere to go.

Dante popped into my mind, but I had too much pride to ask him for help. He'd moved on to someone else. I wasn't on his mind anymore. I could call up my recent lover and ask to spend the night, but that idea made me feel cheap.

It was the first time I was actually scared. Once I was on my own, men would be chasing me. Caspian would try to kill me. I was homeless, so I would be easy to find. I could probably get into the theater and sleep backstage, but that was an obvious place to track me to.

I hadn't wanted to marry Maverick in the first place, but now I realized it was the best thing that had ever happened to me.

He was the man who took care of me.

But I threw that away when I saw those women. I did the right thing and protected the innocent—but I paid a price for it. If I could do it all over again, I probably would have done the same thing. I couldn't live with that guilt—and neither could Maverick. My actions set off terrible repercussions, but there was no other option.

I sat on my bed with my suitcase against the wall. Maverick said I could stay until morning, but I wasn't sure what the point of staying was. It would be easier to sneak into the theater now when people were there. I could stop by and say I forgot something but hide in a closet until everyone went home for the night. There were showers there as well as a couple of cots.

I could make a home there until I figured out what to do next.

It would be okay...right?

A knock sounded on my door before Maverick walked inside.

I glanced at him then turned away, unable to handle the disappointment in his eyes. When his father was strangling him to death, he'd given up like he wanted to die. But once my life was on the line, he did everything he could to protect me—even against his own father.

Maverick sat on the bed beside me, keeping a foot of space in between us.

I stared at the floor. "I've decided to leave now instead of waiting until morning..." I didn't have a car because I gave it to Ramon's wife and daughter. I couldn't afford to waste money on a cab, so I'd have to walk if he wouldn't give me a ride. I'd never felt so helpless in my entire life. I literally had nothing...except for a few hundred bucks.

Maverick was quiet. Maybe he was here because he had the same thought. He didn't want me to be in his house a second longer. "Remember the time I left in the middle of the night to fix a broken pipe on the property?"

I only remembered it because some woman named Becky had made a peculiar entrance while we had breakfast. With her heels in hand, she kissed him on the neck and walked past me, not at all concerned that I was his wife. "Yes."

"That was a lie."

I turned to him, watching the side of his face.

"Your father had made a deal with a man named Kamikaze. Some kind of investment. He came to my front gates to collect you."

My blood turned to ice.

"Said he would turn you into a sex slave to raise the money your father owed him."

I'd been scared to survive on my own, but now I was terrified. This man would hunt me down and force me into prostitution. Now I wished I had a gun so I could blow my brains out. I'd rather die than be subjected to that torture.

"I wouldn't give you up, so he offered to buy you from me." He brought his hands together and stared at his palms. "I told him you weren't for sale—at any price."

I had been dead asleep, and Maverick kept me safe. He didn't even tell me about it, probably because he knew it would disturb me. "Thanks for the heads-up..." Now I realized how much I needed Maverick, that he was the only thing standing in between me and torture.

"You won't survive out there. If Kamikaze doesn't get you, my father will. You won't even last a week."

My hands started to shake because I'd never been this scared in my entire life.

"So, I take back what I said… I'll stay married to you."

I turned to him, surprised he had changed his mind.

He rose to his feet again. "It would be a shame that you saved those girls but there's no one to save you." He headed to the door. "You broke my trust when you snuck around behind my back. You betrayed me when you took matters into your own hands. Don't expect me to trust you again." He opened the door.

I went after him. "Maverick."

He stopped in front of the door. It took him a second to turn around, like he was considering ignoring me.

"Thank you for letting me stay…" If he'd kicked me out on the street, I would have been raped and killed. Changing his mind meant I got to live…and that meant he saved my life. "Without you, I wouldn't have anything. And I realize that now more than ever. You're a good man…and I hope I can earn your forgiveness someday."

His eyes were lifeless, like those words meant nothing to him. "Don't count on it."

ALSO BY PENELOPE SKY

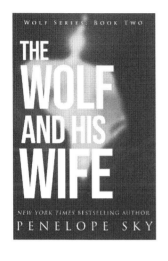

Tensions rise and now I have two enemies that want me dead.

But I've never felt safer.

My wolf protects me. He cherishes me. And I think he loves me.

This arranged marriage was detested by us both, but now I look at him with new eyes.

My husband is strong, smart, and gorgeous. His coffee-colored eyes make me melt. My heart slowly starts to soften for this man and I fall deeper and deeper.

I fall in love with my husband.

Order Now

WANT TO ORDER SIGNED PAPERBACKS?

Would you love a signed copy of your favorite book? Now you can purchase autographed copies and get them sent right to your door!

Get your copy here:

https://penelopesky.com/store

Due to the high volume of submissions, books are only shipped once per month. It may take 6 weeks to received your signed book. US orders only at this time